RESET THE WORLD

Thorns of Life

By

ANDREA BEDFORD

Get a Free Copy of 'Deceive the World'

Your Free Book is Waiting

"Has it ever occurred to you that if you want to survive in this dark world, you have to become darkness itself?

Emilia Wilson was a typical, not so typical, 3rd-year college student who wanted nothing more than to pass all her subjects, read the books she had bought, and enjoy a good cup of her favorite tea in peace.

When she got a phone call from her parents to visit her Grandmother, who was at death's door, Emilia was pulled into the grand scheme of monstrous crimes, and the tea she wished for was nothing more than a long-forgotten dream.

Get a copy of the prequel

Deceive the World: Thorns of Life series here:

ANDREA BEDFORD

www.andreabedford.com[1]

---

1. http://www.andreabedford.com/

Table of Contents

ANDREA BEDFORD

Chain of Chaos 0.

Reasoning I tried
Everything that I knew
Before me.
In my mind
Rationality was no longer valid
This was beyond
Humanity

Chapter 1

Oh, where to start-
Well, I am the reincarnation of the devil, to put it lightly. Or, at
the very least, I have to think of myself that way.
My desire to change the world was no longer as pure as you
would wish it to be. Hey, let's not lie here. It is driven by power.
But, truly, my diary, how can anyone change the world without
losing themselves in their own madness?
How far would you actually be able to go?

That was a broken mess of thoughts that wandered Emilia's mind making her in desperate need to write everything in her diary. She didn't just wonder about anything; she was more of an action person.

And just how much of yourself do you need to sacrifice in order to keep going towards a goal that not just might, but rather has a high-chance of never seeing that perfect world in your lifetime?

How much is it worth?
How much until you are no longer sick of feeling anything?
How much until the numbness kicks in?
How long until a high dose of sleep medication is no longer
needed for one to fall asleep?

How much until you no longer feel anything when you indirectly commit a murder?

That's when her harsh rationality kicked in and told her that she had nothing to lose, so she might as well give up the last of her humanity for a better cause.

One could easily argue she was delusional to think that "cleansing" the world of corruption was even possible.

But then, how do you preserve everything that didn't need to be fixed? How do you proceed *after* everything is destroyed and set anew?

She calmly put the pencil down, her poker expression dimly lit under a candlelight in a small stone room, a full moon being her only night companion. Her mind wandered to that one damned regret that was her constant companion for the following-

Has it truly been 16 years, my little idiot?

The reality of such a number of years started settling in her mind now that she finally thought of it, bringing up a spurge of emotions she was not ready to face.

Sometimes it feels like it's been thousands of years of the same battle, and other times, it feels like yesterday.

And sometimes, just sometimes, I need a reminder of what I am even fighting for.

Why did I even start anything in the first place?

A knock rudely cut off her thoughts, reminding her that there was another human being in the safety bunker there with her in Germany.

"Are you decent, sis?" An all-too-familiar voice spoke, and she found a ghost of a smile playing on her lips, "I brought you something to eat."

Placing the diary in the drawer, she replied, "Of course I am. What the bloody hell do you think I am doing in here?"

The door opened, revealing a young black-haired male in his late twenties adorned in casual attire, his big round eyes closed for a second as he shook his head a little, and with a small smirk on his face, "Better safe than sorry." Sometimes, she would forget that her brother was an adult, and he was no longer in need of her as much as he used to.

But-

Despite his age and the years passing by, he would always remain her baby brother.

His timing couldn't be better. His small cheeky grin reminded Emilia that playfulness and pureness were something that she would protect by *any* means, no matter how seldom he displayed it. She was literally changing the world just to keep it alive, even if it meant becoming a monster in the eyes of so many.

Even if she became a monster in his own eyes.

But if it meant persevering her little (not-so-little) brother's hope (at least what was of it), she was more than willing to sacrifice herself in the process. The bigger the stakes, the bigger the reward.

The tea on the tray reminded her that a certain little idiot couldn't protect herself even if her life depended on it.

Ha, it might be doing the same for her as well.

She eyed the silver tray that her brother had placed on the desk. It was filled with a delicious fish steak, rice covered in a mushroom sauce (Some people just loved the mushroom sauce!) with some veggies on the side, as well as hibiscus tea sweetened just the way she had always preferred.

She immediately dived into the food, relishing in the perfect creamy taste in her mouth, knowing very well that her brother had eaten dinner already.

After all, wasn't the taste in her mouth worth a kill here and there?

She felt his stare slowly becoming too awkward, even by her standards.

"Is everything alright?" he finally asked, his voice low, filled with concern, and she knew that he was eyeing her up and down, "You don't seem to be in any physical pain."

Emilia gave him a ghost of a smile, taking another piece with her fork. The fish was soft, so she didn't need to use the knife at all, "Has anything been alright since they were gone?"

Inwardly, she scowled at the fact that she used the word *gone* rather than the real harsh truth. After all, it was no mystery that their parents were murdered.

Murdered. Killed. Slaughtered.

Anything but fucking gone. It's not like they have gone to the store or work. They were bloody pawns in the game of a monster.

Then again, haven't I become the worst monster that ever was…?

His shoulders tensed a little, but he smiled nonetheless. It was a rather weak smile, the one that you offer someone when you feel utterly helpless and at a loss for words. The one that doesn't even last 3 seconds, "You just look more grim than usual, Emy."

"Please, remind me of the time when I was all sunshine and rainbow."

"The time when you were a child, and…with her.", she tsked at him, still chewing the last bite, "To be honest, knowing that at least you're so close to her this time, I thought it would do something positive to you considering…everything."

She gave him an odd look, and this time the smile on his face reached his eyes.

"But...despite everything, I think you need to be reminded that you can stop...It's been over 15 years of you going around the world, executing some sort of twisted justice, and I...You can stop, Emy. For your own good."

"Stopping is not even an option at this point."

"Why?" He clutched his hands, "Why won't you just tell the world the truth? Why do you insist on going with *this*?" his voice was firm, but she very well noticed the little tremble it held for that mini-, no, nanosecond, indicating all the grief behind.

She closed her eyes, slowly swallowing her food along with all her feelings. Or, at the very least, what was left of them, "You know that you can always leave and that even then, I would protect you at all costs. You would live like a king despite anything."

The man let out a deep sigh, his hands crossed, "Do you seriously think that after everything, I could ever go on living.... a normal life? Truth be told, I am not even sure what a normal life is anymore."

"..." her silence was like an agreement to his statement. *Normal* was not an option for either of them in every sense of the word. Both of them would continue going in their own ways, just like moonlight would always creep into her bunker in Germany...or any other one she owned.

"But I know that I can't let you be on your own." He quickly added with a small chuckle, "Powerful, intelligent, and messed up in every way? A chaotic combo indeed." Turning around, he stared into her eyes intensely, but she quickly swallowed the guilt that was skulking somewhere in the depths of her mind, "I just want you to be happy. But, sis, don't you see that everything you are trying to create is destroying you as well?"

"You could never understand anything because you have always been a better person than I am. Don't you think I already know that? But all the same, the very same power that keeps destroying me is the one that keeps me going. Fascinating, is it?" a sorrowful smile made its way to her face, "It eats you alive, but it makes you feel alive."

Rocky stayed silent, awkwardly standing in the place, his eyes silently judging her, but he spoke no more, giving up entirely on that conversation.

"Why are we even back in Germany after...so long? I thought that it's something we agree on...that nothing good happens in Germany; not to us at least."

Still eating her meal, she found herself searching for an answer. The true reason was...not something she could ever possibly share with him. After all, the reality of that reason was unsettling-

No

Unsettling would be an understatement of the century

I, out of everyone, should know better. Should know that humanity is capable of bringing doomsday because too much power and knowledge is never a good thing.

"The usual. You really don't want to know the details. This is my shit to worry about, not yours."

After all, it is I who decided to give my last gift to humanity. To give up my own in order to cleanse the world. Better yet, reset the current one.

Chapter 2

That night was one of those nights when she had to use an unhealthy amount of sleeping medications in order to even have a slim chance of actually falling asleep. At first, they had worked like a miracle but just like with anything artificial, her body...got used to it more and more until she had to swallow them like candies because those little chemicals were the only thing she could turn to when her mind refused to keep quiet.

After all, those little friends were the strongest sleeping medication known to mankind at that moment.

This is my shot in history. I truly wonder how I will be interpreted by future generations.

That is if there is a future one considering all the data that I possess?

Pulling out the diary that was under her pillow, she yawned, her body bathing in the moonlight that was allowed to get inside the tiny window at the top of the ceiling. After all, it was a bunker hidden deep in the forest, and that tiny window was her only source of the real outside world there in Germany.

She lay comfortably in her bed as one of her hands went up, playing with the strings of moonlight that caressed her body. It was a small satisfaction in nature's beauty that she still held dearly, embracing the loneliness of the night. She reached for her diary that was under the pillow (yeah, she needed to hide it better from Rocky), and soon as her hands felt the fluffy cover, she pulled it out and traced through the soft fabric.

Fluff, fluff, fluff

That thought made her giggle for a second, but nonetheless, she opened it eventually.

It's fascinating how writing down your thoughts can help a person to keep their mind on the right path and remind them why they are doing whatever it may be.

Subconsciously, she flipped to the first pages when she started writing down her thoughts and the whole experience in the first place. For a moment, she thought that every single experience following the death of her parents was nothing more than a living nightmare. It was an odd experience, to say at least. Not only would her mind disassociate with reality, but her body as well. She would look at her bloody hands, and she could swear they weren't hers. She would look at her exhausted expression in the mirror and not be able to recognize that that person was her.

Or, as Emilia wrote inside the journal 15 years ago.

Just me, myself, and I.
After all, who else could there be?

Perhaps, she just played her part way well, even for her good.

But then again, if I hadn't, then I would not be here alive.

The memories of her nights in the criminal asylum crept in, and for a moment, she thought she truly belonged in that place.

Confused?

Oh, so was she those 15 bloody years ago when she saw on the news that she, apparently, **was** the Demon of the Night.

Ah, Germany. Why do you hate me so much?

She hadn't watched the live news but saw it whilst scrolling through the news the morning after. She remembered being in such a state of shock that she just kept staring at the screen of her phone in that same bunker, in the same room that she was currently occupying. Just staring right through the phone as though if she had stared enough, the reality would disappear.

However, the reality was everything but merciful.

What comes next when the whole world is against you?

. . .

I couldn't let the true Demon go unpunished.

I had to play the devil's game.

No.

I had to become worse than everyone.

Her brother didn't believe the fake news at all, but he was in an opposite state than she was. She stared at him with a small wicked smile whilst he panicked that she would be executed if she just stepped right out of the bunker that was probably made centuries ago and hid secrets that she had no idea about.

Smile, smile, smile

And fool the world

She was pretty proud of the fact that she came up with a plan on how to "get away" with everything. Although, after listening to her plan, Rocky remained silent and said that she truly was insane, that the plan was risky, and had way too many variables.

Emilia...agreed. But she had no choice but to play her role convincingly; she played the insanity card until everyone was her fool and until she started believing her own lies.

At some points, I would argue that I perhaps didn't need to lie.

I was broken in every way you could think of.

After all, how can one remain sane in this world?

"I will be everyone's fool but little did they know they were all my fools." She read out aloud one of the lines from the diary, smiling to herself, a weird sense of pride wriggling inside her.

What truly happened 15 years go after she left Sophia and got reunited with her brother?

She followed any clues that she possibly could that could trace her back to the Demon and his little pawns. What better place to start than to get all the documentations that her father had and everything he had managed to find. She remembered a wave of regret for never telling her father how proud she truly was of him. They may have had their differences, but deep down, she respected his abilities a great deal.

In a way, she was a reflection of him when it came to work. It never mattered how many jobs and how long; what mattered was getting them done your way because you *knew* your worth. Getting it done properly.

Of course, she respected her mother the same deal, but... there is always that one parent that got you just a spec more, creating a certain understanding in between.

So, she got everything she possibly could (at this point, she already had found this bunker) and got back in contact with the same Russian girl that "helped" Sophia and her during their time in Africa.

The part of her that might not have been okay with using the money of the man that Sophia and her had found on that cruise was long gone.

She only had one goal in mind; revenge.

Utter revenge and destruction of everything that Demon had. Means did not matter a tiny bit. Her rage and grief were stronger than her morals ever were.

During that period, Rocky stayed with their relatives.

She remembered using so much caffeine that, at some point, there were days that she would go without sleeping or eating...and drinking unless energy drinks and pills counted.

It didn't take a while to finish the very step of what her father was going on about that evening when Sophia and Alice came to dinner. Or was it lunch? Either way...her father was unaware that there was an insider in the investigation. Someone who was covering up the crucial parts of the investigation, keeping up with everything but letting the detectives know *just enough* to keep the game going.

Surprise, surprise, ladies and gentlemen, it was no other than Alice bloody Stein, the father's assistant. How cliché was that?

Her father had found out about it, but...he was late. At this point, Alice was done playing her role.

> *But no one was aware of the new player.*
> *So I paid a little visit to her.*

> ...

> *At what point does revenge taste sweet?*

Emilia laid down on her bed, turning on a side, still reading some parts of the diary here and there. She skipped the pages that went on about her visit to Alice...and her very first indirect murder. The initial feeling of regret was long gone as well.

After all, a murderer can never be happy.

After that...she took everything she could from Alice that was useful (although Alice was quite cooperative) and carried on her revenge. Emilia yawned, closing her eyes for a few seconds, remembering Ronald's face when she pulled the gun.

That was sweet.

Oh, so so sweet. The one that executed my parents and so many others.

The Demon's right-hand man.

But then, why did I cry if it was so sweet?

How come the rain couldn't wash away any of my sins?

It was only a few hours after she executed Ronald that she found out about her "becoming" the Demon.

Chapter 3

*"I am the Demon of Munich. The Devil. The one that you have been looking for so long. So then, Emilia Wilson, what are you waiting for? Shoot." The man, no, scratch that, the **boy** said, grinning ever so slightly at her with joy but deeply rooted pain.*

"Why? Why do you smile whilst looking right at death?"

The boy tilted his head slightly; the grin on his face was disappearing, his piercing blue eyes clouded with something that made her shiver,

"Death…is the only thing I can look forward to."

Emilia opened her mouth, shocked at the answer, unsure what to ask the boy that could only be a few years older than her own baby brother.

"You could say I am the perfect mistake of humanity's wickedness."

"Elaborate." She said in a firm voice but the one that held some dose of maternal instinct at the boy that was more and more resembling her own brother in front of her eyes. Her eyes were unfocused at the moment that she had been anticipating for so long; the bittersweet revenge.

"Why does it matter to you? You are going to kill me." He smiled slightly, and for a moment, she wanted to smile back at the mutual understanding of their pain. For a split second, she thought that in

another life, they might have been close friends, "Certainly, you wouldn't come this far just talk to me, right?"

"For the love of life, just answer. You literally have nothing to lose. I mean, either way, I am taking everything you have created. Or better yet, destroyed."

"I just wanted someone to understand my pain," he said, his voice melancholic, perfectly matching his eyes that illuminated the lack of fire or any emotion. "I knew you would come. Perhaps in your moral compass, everything is so wrong, but the fact that it is right to me, and it is a good enough reason."

"You know...normal people usually talk to a therapist or someone."

"Then what about you?"

Tsk...the little bastard. He got her there.

"Will you continue playing this game? Why would you want to know? You don't care about anyone but yourself."

She narrowed her eyes a tiny bit, searching for anything in the Devil's eyes, but she found nothing. Those were like a wasteland with no sign of life, "You're right. I don't care...but I will understand."

"..."

Emilia let out a small sigh, "A murderer can never be happy. I want to know your reasons. I want to know more about what makes you...you."

And so... the Devil talked to her for hours. Talked about every single wicked desire he had had. About his past. About his eternal grief.

About him.

*And about **her**.*

The sun didn't wake her up, but the fact that she had to use the bathroom rather urgently. She stumbled onto the cold floor and mentally thanked the fact that she still had her socks on, which led her to another conclusion whilst she slowly made her way to the bathroom.

She actually slept through the night!

She didn't remember how or when; she was too lost in re-reading her own thoughts from the diary, and at some point, she just lost her consciousness. Once she finished using the bathroom, she went back to bed despite the fact that she knew she would not be able to fall asleep again.

However, she felt rested to some point; after all, anything is better than sleepless nights. She looked at the clock and realized it was 11 in the morning. She realized she had slept for solid eight and a half hours without waking up at all.

Nice.

She remembered that she was reading her diary before falling asleep and subconsciously looked around it; however, she found nothing on her bed, and soon after, she found it on the ground near her bed. She reached for it from her bed and mentally thanked the fact that it was close.

She wasn't ready yet to get out of bed.

But if she was frank with herself, she hasn't been ready for the last 10 years.

"So what exactly is the plan? I mean, you probably don't plan on staying inside the bunker the whole time." Her brother said, crossing his arms over his chest with a small tilt of his head, "And yet...ever since we came back to Germany, you don't really...do anything. Is everything alright, Emy?"

She didn't look at him but rather made a small 'hmm' sound.

"It's...just very complicated. That's all. I am thinking of our next move because I have lost a very useful member of the group."

Whilst her brother was familiar that she had a small organization of very few skilled members, he wasn't aware of who exactly the members were, nor did he really understand Emilia's goal. Perhaps no one really did.

Rocky took a sip of his hot chocolate and made a small nod, "And what happened to this person?"

He killed himself.

FYI, this person is also the murderer of our parents, and yet I gave him his favorite sweet treat before he ended himself.

As you can see, I am trying my best to be the better person here.

"He..." Emilia let out a small laugh, "fulfilled his deepest desire, and decided to be selfish for the second time in his life."

Her brother gave her a confused look and shrugged his shoulders. After so many years, he was just used to the fact that Emilia was never going to truly let him know everything. He will always be her little brother, not that he was ungrateful.

After all, there wasn't a single time in their lives when she didn't fulfill her promise to him.

Even the smallest ones.

"But there has to be something...."

Emilia continued eating her breakfast, closing her eyes for a moment. She did a lot when she was thinking. It was easier to isolate herself in her mind than to face the cruel reality that was unfolding.

"Perhaps, if things come to their worst, I have an idea of what to do." She finally answered after a short pause that she deemed to be a little too dramatic.

Damn, those eggs and ham are hella delicious!

"And that is…?" Rocky raised his eyebrows a little, curious and satisfied that his sister was sharing at least something with him.

"Live"

It made perfect sense to both of them.

Chapter 4

L ive.
    To live.

What did it even mean anymore?

A distant memory of the definition crossed her mind from the Thesaurus that her parents had had.

Remain alive.

She despised that definition, for how all the wonders of the living world could be summed up in two words was *beyond* her. Only the fools would be satisfied with *that* definition.

How do you live when you know that the world war is slowly approaching?

How do you...stop the inevitable?

Emilia starred at the screen of her laptop (technically not truly hers), not even sure what to think or how to feel at the results and reports of the collective efforts of Daniel's last work as well as her own research. Oh! And the Russian girl. She would always forget her name. Oh, those Russians are so efficient in technology.

The first person that she thought of was her brother. She wasn't particularly worried for herself; evil always survives in some form.

She closed her eyes as she held in the emotions, except that she wasn't fully sure what she was holding in the first place.

She didn't feel fear or dread. Of course, it wasn't happiness either. She didn't want the world to end.

Oh, the end? She knew that humanity had too much power for its good.

And living on Mars wasn't an option yet.

But...Emilia did feel like a giant failure in her own eyes. The one thing was that the only good side of the goal she worked for was no longer achievable. The peaceful world for people like her baby brother or her little idiot was no longer available.

She stood up in slow motion and approached the wall that was next to her. She hit it hard. She hit all of the emotions that were sucking her into the deep abyss inside, the only fire that kept her alive all those years. A few sobs escaped her, and she was left with a pile of tears running down her eyes because, deep down, she knew this was the end; that this was the limit of how much power she truly had, and that no amount of wickedness could keep her running towards a goal that she had in her deepest and darkest dream.

The dream where criminals were non-existent, where the government actually cared for the citizens, and where the over-population alongside its cons was not a thing. A world that would be created by her own hands, albeit filled with bitter-sweet blood and her mockery at the systems that kept up the rich getting richer whilst the poor kept being poorer with every following generation.

You know, the usual dreams that people had.

She noticed the dirt and blood on her hands which made her smile a little.

At least she cleaned this corrupted and rotten world a little. She did her own share of things.

Even though the world would still choke in its own misery, it was still...nice knowing she finished her life homework despite the fact that she still didn't have a full grasp on the material.

Ha!

As if...

As if she ever stood a chance against the world!

She was just a measly little human with too many ambitions and wickedness for her good.

Sophia!

It hit her like a thousand bricks that her little idiot could not survive on her own.

Hell, unlike Emilia, Sophia was too kind for her own good. Too kind to the world that never knew how to appreciate it.

Emilia looked up through the small window. She smiled to herself and thought of the other dreams she had somewhere in the deepest parts of her mind, buried so far that she could not even reach for them herself.

She didn't dare to think of them too much.

"Live"

Chapter 5

"Soon, we are going to have some company." Emilia declared to her brother with a neutral face, and soon as the realization hit her, she could not help but smile a little. It was a small genuine feeling of longing that was so warm and welcoming that she thought she didn't deserve it.

"Oh? And may I know who?" Richard looked up from the game that he was playing on the tablet with surprise written all over his face.

"Oh, you know. The little idiot that was my partner for so long. We all had dinner before we disappeared. She saved our Granny's life too." She sat down, sighing a little as the memories flooded back to her. She was yet to tell why she would be their new roommate.

Well, more like bunkermate.

"Well, that is...certainly surprising news. But, Emy, you do know that going outside in public is always risky, no matter how careful you are."

"I know, but that's for sure the world's least problem." She gave him a sarcastic pouty face, trying to approach the subject gently, "We all are kinda in a tough spot."

"Tough as in getting worse politically and economically?"

"Tough as in...every possible sense of that world. Tough as in..." she stopped herself as soon as she saw her brother waiting for her answer with that childish glint that he always had in his eyes despite everything.

What good would it be for him to know what would happen when neither of them could possibly do anything to protect any of the mundane routines that they had left of, anything that resembled, at last, a slice of a normal life?

So she gave him a grin and winked at him, "Well, I guess you are right. The usual shit."

Richard made a small "mhm" sound and indulged himself back in his game. Emilia knew that Richard probably didn't trust her answer but already knew that he would not get any further answers. He probably had learned by now that sometimes his sister would lie, even to him, just so she would protect him in any way she could.

He loved it and hated it at the same time.

He looked at her properly when he finished the level of his game and was surprised by the sight before him. His sister had a faraway look, and he knew that she was probably deep in thought, but that wasn't the unusual part.

The odd part was her smile. It was a small but kind and genuine smile that he remembered seeing a long time ago when his sister still had her humanity with her.

"Oh, Emy...what an idiot you have been...if only...you just weren't too ambitious for your own good." He whispered to himself, knowing very well that that source of happiness for his sister was so obvious, but perhaps, at the time, he was too young to understand.

Maybe there was still hope for Emilia in some form. Not the kind that you could buy with money, but rather the kind that brings you back from the depths of the abyss of despair that Emilia had gotten herself into. It's not that she didn't have faith in humanity; rather, she refused to give up that this world was broken beyond repair. It was rather paradoxical.

She didn't put faith in anyone but herself, and yet, ultimately, everything that she has been doing was for the sake of humanity itself. But, somewhere along the lines, she forgot that she belonged to humanity *as well*, and there was only one person who was able to contradict everything that Emilia deemed to be true.

Sophia Wilson, the woman that didn't waltz but crushed into her life so unexpectedly and rocked Emilia's entire life. One of the kindest people that existed. Perhaps the kindest one.

Richard was blessed with that fact.

"I am looking forward to having Sophia with us." He said softly and grinned like a Cheshire cat at the red-headed woman who, for the first time in a while, grinned back at him.

Chapter 6

A few weeks had passed since Emilia had told her brother about Sophia, but meanwhile, some shit happened, *like always*, and she basically found herself recklessly running toward the graveyard where she knew that Sophia would be. Well, more like traced her easily.

Damn, the drizzle was annoying.

The world was annoying.

She ran through the forest as fast as her legs were able to carry her, and at some point, the wind against her skin became hurtful, but she didn't mind it. Or rather, she didn't have time to mind it.

As though some silly wind could bring her down.

As soon as that thought entered her mind, she got trapped over a random branch but managed to land on her now bruised hands, and she was up in a matter of seconds, not allowing the forest to swallow her.

Shit, I know I am close-

But would she be able to get there in time? This is a question she didn't dare to think of.

She **had** to. She couldn't possibly allow Sophia to be killed when she had the means to save her.

Emilia wanted to take a break too badly and allow her lungs some much-needed oxygen, but she couldn't stop now!

Oxygen is so overrated.

Fuck it, Sophia. I hate your dependency on others!

I hate your kindness!

I hate how much of a weakling you are!

But...

I could never hate you, my darling idiot.

Rain washed away all of her deepest desires, and she took out the special gun that she had for her. Rain and glasses was certainly an awful combo.

"Answer me, you sophisticated container!" Emilia suddenly heard in the near distance, and without thinking, she moved her body in that direction to the all-familiar voice of everything that needed to be protected just so somewhere deep inside, she could tell herself that there was a chance.

What the...A chance for what...?

"For fuck sake, answer me why! Why do you need to kill us?!"

Ah, there was her little idiot.

Partner...I am not saying goodbye to you.

Emilia raised the gun and closed one of her eyes to improve her aim. After all, she had done this so many times that at this point, it was her second nature to shoot, whichever gun she was given.

The shoot was silent and a bit anti-climactic, in her opinion, but it did the job, and finally, she was able to take a deep breath of oxygen that she had been craving so much.

Her partner was safe.

Good...that's good.

However, she remembered the warnings of one of her allies and shouted, "Don't move!" without too much thinking. Emilia approached the humanoid-looking robot and quickly shot it at the precise locations that her Russian ally had told her about.

She let out a sigh in relief that that went without any problems, but as soon as she looked around, she realized that the man on the cold cement was most probably dead, and not only that-

She knew him. Not personally, and truth to be told, she didn't care about him too much, but he was still a part of her secret group, and-

"Fuck, he has a kid- fuck."

Emanuel...a man that, at times, reminded Emilia of her own father, whom she also failed to protect.

But she swallowed all of her feelings, numbing them down just like she always did, and placed the gun in the holder inside her cloak, and finally, she turned around to her forever-partner, and her eyes instantly softened upon seeing the pitiful but beautiful figure kneeling down on the ground staring right back at her with eyes full of disbelief and joy. Emilia knelt down on Sophia's level and fought back every urge to hug her until the end of the time; instead, she gently placed her hands on Sophia's shoulders, hoping that her own partner was kind enough to understand that words were meaningless at the moment.

For a moment, it was just the two of them again, and Emilia thought that the world might as well disappear right then and there because Sophia was in her arms.

Just like the good ol' days.

Except...the cold rain and the sorrow in which both of them were drowning reminded them that nothing was like good ol' times.

Sophia swallowed a lump in her throat and made a grimace which Emilia wasn't sure to think of because, for a moment, she was worried about Sophia's mental state rather than hers.

So, just like in the good ol' days, she remained calm and rational by saying, "We have to go. *Quickly!* Not sure if there are others around."

"Em..." Sophia muttered with so much pain that Emilia squeezed her partner's shoulders as a micro sign of reassurance.

Emilia continued speaking the same words over and over, telling her that they desperately needed to go to safety and that being here, exposed in the rain, was not good for anyone.

However, the brunette woman just kept shaking her head rapidly as if she was in a trance, repeating Emilia's nickname over and over until it was louder and borderline nuts for her.

She even appeared to be the sane one in this situation.

Seems like the world has done a great deal of pain to her too.

A loud slap filled the air, and Emilia knew that that slap was good enough to bring Sophia back to some resemblance of sanity, albeit the fact that she hated that she had to do it in the first place.

But what choice did she have?!

Sophia's eyes widened in shock, and one of her hands slowly went upwards, trailing the red spot on her cheek, staring right into Emilia's own green eyes, which made Emilia's insides protest for not reaching out and just tell Sophia everything that was on her soul despite the dance macabre that both of them were doing with the world.

She wished she had enough courage to kiss the spot where she had slapped her.

Sophia took a good look at Emilia, and she noticed the most time she spent staring at her were her eyes which resulted in Emilia smiling on the inside but keeping the strict façade outside.

"Look, I get it! Your mom is dead; I was at the funeral, albeit hiding between the trees; your boyfriend just died; and I am back from the dead by killing that sophisticated container, which by the way, is a great description of them, and I am proud of you! Additionally, I know the dead guy was a great person, and yes, it's fucking unfortunate, and I wish I could have saved him too, but we have to go somewhere else. This place might not be safe." She made sure her words had a sharp edge to them just so Sophia would fully understand the seriousness of the situation that she probably knew nothing of.

"He might still be alive...." Sophia let out a sob, placing a hand where Emilia slapped her, which due to the cold rain, was probably burning. Maybe it wasn't even the rain; perhaps it was the fact that Emilia *herself* had to raise a hand on her.

The world has changed so much but not you...
You are still the best person I have known.

"I am not a nurse like you, but he's dead. That shot went right through his heart, and he lost a lot of blood." Emilia replied grimly, taking a glance at Emanuel's body. "Fuck. Let's just get out of here."

In the depths of her mind, she imagined a better reunion. After all, the bond that they shared was unique on so many levels that neither of them was fully able to understand, and she only wished that the universe would someday, at some better time, give them what both of them searched for.

Sophia, this is not normal, but it's us.
It's not goodbye until we say so.

Chapter 7

You know those times when things just fell right where they belonged? When the pieces just perfectly fit like they had never been apart in the first place.

For Sophia, taking Emilia's soft hand and following her was the most natural state of her being that she could think of when she so abruptly jumped back into her life.

It was more than abrupt. It was like the fastest train hit her out of nowhere, leaving her in a state of...dark reality and a-dreamless state-of-mind that she had buried long...looooong time ago.

"His kid...is at home?" Emilia suddenly asked, leaning against the tree, still holding Sophia's hand firmly, "How old is she? Do you know where he lives?"

For a moment, Sophia looked around, realizing that they were deeper in the forest and that, in the meantime, the rain was nowhere near its end, which as dramatic as it sounded, Sophia felt like it just escalated the eerie feeling of the atmosphere which forest would give her. The fact that she had no idea of what was going on was not helping either.

Nadine!

Sophia snapped out of her trance, nodding a little even though Emilia wasn't looking at her but rather at the ground, her eyes focused on nothing in particular as though...she was emphatic?

But Sophia clicked her tongue a little, remembering that this was Emilia. Emphatic and Emilia didn't go together. She was one of the most, if not *the most* egotistic person she knew.

And yet, over and over, Sophia would go to the end of the world with her.

Why?

Why do I refuse to say goodbye to her?

"Um, yes. Where else would she be? I also...happen to be her friend. Oh, yeah! She is a teen." She bit her bottom lip and let out a long sigh, "Em...what the *fuck* is going on?"

Emilia's presence certainly made her gain some confidence that came out of nowhere.

But at that moment, any feeling was better than the initial shock, sorrow, and fear sprinkled with just a dash of anger.

This time, her red-headed partner looked at her and smiled bitterly. She opened her mouth for a moment, but then Sophia realized that Emilia was contemplating doing something-

Which apparently, she decided not to and closed her mouth.

Finally, she let out a deep sigh and looked at Sophia sternly, "I will take you to a safe space and then bring that kid."

"I am coming with you!" Sophia replied without a moment of hesitation, tears appearing in the corners of her eyes once again, "It's the least I can do. Besides, you really think she is going to follow a stranger?"

"I want you to be safe, my darling idiot. But, it appears that the way you treat others hasn't changed-" Emilia gave her a kind smile, "It's beautiful."

For a split millisecond, Sophia thought that Emilia created the world where only the two of them existed, where the cruel reality couldn't get them, and everything was perfect, and-

Sophia's insides did a long-forgotten twist, but the good kind, and once again, she started seeing something familiar in those green eyes.

Sophia was bashful for a moment and decided to look down, "It's—not just that. Emanuel and Nadine are my friends. Well...he *was* my friend. He *saved* me—Oh god!"

Suddenly, the very fact that *that* world did not exactly hit her, and the harsh truth of their positions swallowed her, and being overwhelmed by everything, she pulled her hands up, sobbing into them, breaking the hand contact with Emilia.

"How could-" she hiccupped a little, wiping away her tears, "I possibly face Nad-" but she couldn't even finish her sentence without sobbing, "ine.."

"Being a sobbing mess is not going to help. You are not the one to blame. He decided to save you, for which I am eternally going to be grateful, but right now, Nadine will need you to comfort her, not vice versa, so pull yourself together. If not for the sake of egoism, then for Nadine." Emilia stated as though she was at some conference, "You are right. I will need your help to bring Nadine safe and sound without struggling."

Sophia was not surprised by the cold rationality on Emilia's part; from the very beginning, this was the core of her being, and she even warned her quite a number of times that nothing would ever change about it.

To someone else, Emilia might have sounded like a cold-hearted egotistical bitch who thought she knew the best but-

The reality was that Emilia cared a little too much for her own liking and that she was hiding behind her own egoism more than she would ever admit.

"You know very well that I am right." She added and turned around, smiling at Sophia slightly, giving her a well-known look with her hand offered, "Partner."

And the last word struck Sophia deeper than she thought it would, and she could not help but make a grimace that comforted into happiness, something that was utterly morbid of her to feel at the moment.

She took Emilia's soft hand in her hands and gave her a small grin, "You know the answer damn well, *partner*."

Chapter 8

Had I known the answer, just one event would have turned our lives in a completely opposite direction.

Ah, my darling idiot, it seems as though the world is getting to you too...

But if I get to see your true smile at the end, then it's worth trying until I succeed.

Truth be told, I am not even sure what I am trying to achieve with you because, ultimately, I can't beat the reality of this one.

But hey, giving up is not in my dictionary, so we are going to...keep going in this one for as long as we can.

That is, I will; you will just tag along.

Emilia smiled at that thought and instructed Sophia to be hidden until the random old man that was passing by Nadine's house was long gone, and with him being gone out of sight, the two women quickly got inside with ease because Sophia had a spare key.

Good news, though!

Rain stopped.

Emilia didn't look around too much but rather decided to follow Sophia into the living room, where she noticed the petite-looking girl with purple hair and strands of blue, which perfectly meddled with the unusual combo. However, it suited her rather cutely, and she even thought that "normal" looking colors could never possibly suit someone *like* her.

Suddenly, the petite girl noticed them, and as soon as her eyes met Sophia, she offered her a huge childish grin, and then her eyes drifted to Emilia, at which her grin didn't disappear, but it was a bit shyer.

"Phia! You didn't tell me you would bring a friend." She smiled kindly and immediately turned around, taking out the cookies from the oven, and carefully placing them on a big round blue plate. She left them on the counter and approached Sophia, who was just staring at the girl without blinking, "Um...Sophia? Earth to Sophia?" she waved in front of her eyes which finally snapped the brunette out of her thoughts, "You are soaking wet! And you too! Ah, how rude of me? I am Nadine."

Emilia offered her a small smile and took the small hand in hers, "Emilia."

"That's a very beautiful name. It's nice to meet you, Em! And- I adore your hair! Red but intense, and that hairstyle- Sooo cool!" Nadine squealed a little, still smiling, and for a moment, Emilia thought they would need to postpone the bad news as much as she could because she couldn't possibly tell her that her father had been killed.

She had been in her place.

It's not just ugly. It's an earth-shattering place where you feel the most vulnerable and the most lonely you could possibly be.

Emilia took Sophia's hand in her own, smiling at the petite girl, "Say, is it fine if we change first? I don't want to catch a cold."

"Of course, Sophia can borrow you some clothes. I will try to call dad in the meantime."

"Alright." The red-headed woman nodded at her without too much thinking, knowing very well that they needed to get away from the petite girl for just a while.

They went back to the hallway, and Emilia decided to get inside the room on the right, which ended up being the correct way because as soon as she saw the room from every anime fan's dream, she knew it *had* to belong to Nadine.

She quickly closed the door behind her and looked at the ceiling, closing her eyes.

Sophia covered her cries with her hands, and her body slowly slid down, her hands muffling her cries. Quickly, she swallowed deep with deep breaths and wiped the tears away with her sleeves.

Emilia looked at her and decided to sit on the bed right before Sophia, "This world hasn't been nice to you...."

Sophia looked up, staring right into her eyes with grief, "That's irrelevant....I...don't matter. Not as much as Nadine does."

The red-headed blinked intensely a few times, staring right back into the messy brunette, "What do you mean?"

"You don't know her as much as I do but Em—She is the most optimistic person that I know. Despite the fact that the odds were against her so many times, she never gave up - Not once! She even—"Sophia smiled bitterly, "saved me...from myself. She goes on living, chasing her dreams, albeit the fact that the world is—just so much against her. With so much pain on her shoulders already, how can I possibly tell her that her own father, whom she adores, is dead?!"

"It's not like you killed him. It's that robot. It's...oh god, it's *so* messed up." Emilia muttered the last part, sighing a little, "Even if she is as strong-willed as you say, what makes you think you are any less important?"

Sophia clutched her hands and looked down at the ground, "Because—I don't contribute to this world at all! In the grand scheme of things, I just...live. Live for myself. Nadine makes this world a little happier place, and we genuinely need more people like her...like *you*. Whether I am alive or dead, it doesn't make any difference."

Emilia's stomach was a little upside down, and she thought of how ridiculous her body was behaving, but she couldn't help the fact that feeling vulnerable with Sophia was worse than killing so many.

And yet, she has grown to love that feeling.

That long-forgotten feeling of longing.

God damnit, I only wish for you to be happy one day.

"You truly are an idiot like you always have been." Emilia tch-ed and rolled her eyes, narrowing her eyes slightly, placing one of her hands under Sophia's chin which made her stare right into her after so long, "Doesn't make a difference? Do you realize the extent of everything I have done for you because I know how much you help the world to be just a little kinder? The dream job that you got so easily with a decent salary was because of *me*. Don't ask how. It's better if you don't know. You stealing the meds for your mom? That Russian girl in my group helped you so many times to avoid being caught on camera, and you? You don't think that *any* of that matters?"

Sophia wasn't sure what to think or feel at that moment. Everything that Emilia said just made her have a thousand and one more questions for her, and yet, now, with at least one explanation, a part of her life finally made more sense.

But even so, another pressing problem at that moment was the fact that Emilia was *able* to do all of that just for her.

How did Emilia gain this much power? Moreover, what exactly was she doing all these years, and why would she come back right when a random robot from what seemed like a scene in a sci-fi book attacked both Emanuel and her?

After being gone for so many years, Sophia, as much of an idiot as she was, according to Emilia, thought that the timing was a little too convenient.

But with Emilia's intense stare at that moment, Sophia backed away from asking any questions and realized that Emilia didn't have to do any of that for her, yet- she was there. She had been in her shadow for so long without her realizing that she had never been truly alone.

"But don't think I was there the whole time." Emilia's hands slowly started sliding off Sophia's face, her face morphing into a small smile of sadness as though she was able to read her thoughts. "At some point, I needed to let you go, and... move on."

Sophia made a small "huh" sound, staring right at Emilia's own eyes, confusion filling her mind, "But-"

"But what?"

"It doesn't make sense...." Sophia narrowed her eyes, clutching her hands at her knees, "Because...Some time ago, I realized! I realized what you wished to tell me on that rainy night!"

Emilia's eyes widened, and she bit her lips a little, glancing around the room, anywhere but Sophia's own eyes. She couldn't stand the intense pressure of Sophia's own brown poles.

"So what?" Emilia finally decided to speak, "It's not like it matters. At least...not in this world."

"And you call *me* an idiot? How on earth have you not realized by now that you will always matter to me! Fuck the world! You are truly never going to be satisfied. You will always just chase something because you will always be ridiculously ambitious. Or better yet, *ambitchous*."

Emilia sat agape for a moment, looking like a deer in headlights at Sophia's sudden outburst, and when her words finally settled in, she wasn't sure whether to feel loved and flattered or angry at such a *factual* insult.

She opened her mouth a little but decided against it, lowering her head a little along with her voice, "Don't... do *not* ever think it's because I wanted to. It was a necessary need for your own good rather than my own wish. Truth be told, it was the only time when I decided not to be selfish."

A sudden knock on the door interrupted their conversation or argument, whatever it may be, and both of them glanced at the door, realizing that this was not a time or place for catching up on the unspoken.

Chapter 9

"So, I have made some tea, but it seems I am interrupting something?" Nadine entered the room a second after knocking, and due to the initial shock, neither Sophia nor Emilia replied to the petite girl.

She had a tray with the four cups on it, and as soon as Sophia saw their design, her eyes widened a little, and she felt a chill running down her spine. At this point, it wasn't the cold or the wet clothes either.

It was those strawberry-looking cups that she was regularly drinking from with Emanuel and Nadine.

"Why four?" Emilia blurted out, attempting to clean her eye glasses with the wipes that she had in her pocket.

Sheesh, she really had no chill.

Sophia lowered her head, focused on her breathing as Nadine put the tray on the desk, and decided to lean her back on the closet.

She offered Emilia one of her usual small and gentle smiles, "Dad should be home soon too. I can't reach him on the phone, but I know how long it takes him when he goes out."

"I see," Emilia murmured, still attempting to wipe her glasses from the damned rain.

"So, Em? May I know how did you two meet?" Nadine asked.

"Oh, that...is a long story. Look, I am not here to chat with you. You don't know me, and I don't know you. But...I know your father...from work." Emilia crossed her legs, adjusted her glasses, and let out a deep sigh in exhaustion, "I need you and Sophia to come with me. It's something your dad would want."

"What?" Nadine looked at Sophia in confusion but received no answer, "What on earth are you talking about?"

"I understand this doesn't make any sense to you right now, but please, I promise to explain everything later. Damn, I still hate making promises."

It's not fair of me to let Em all the hard talk. I need to be strong...just this once.

Sophia looked up and nodded at Nadine, trying her best to give her a kind smile without bursting out again, "I get you are confused, as I am with a lot of stuff, but I know I can trust Em. She...is my partner."

"Your lover?" Nadine immediately raised her eyebrows a little, and a little smirked crossed her features.

"No. Em is my partner in life. Partner in crime. Partner in everything...simply saying, *partner*. My rock...and ultimately, one of the most important people in my life despite disappearing for so god damn *long*!" Finally, Sophia felt something snapping in her, and just like the Prince woke up sleeping beauty with a kiss, a part of Sophia woke up and stood up angrily, planting a slam on Emilia's cheek, "You dare to call me an idiot, and yet, you're the biggest idiot I have ever known!"

The red-headed girl sat there in shock and amusement, staring right into Sophia's clouded eyes as if snapped into some sort of trance. A trance of guilt and longing.

"And if we are ever reborn, let me go back to *that* night!"

The tension was almost eatable.

"Um, I...have no idea what you two are talking about. Both of you *clearly* have some issues to work on." But before Nadine could make another step, Sophia stopped her by grabbing her hand.

"Don't worry about this. It's just so much unimportant at this moment. Excuse my behavior...I just had a very long day. Let's just follow Emilia's lead. I promise we can trust her."

"Just pack everything that you care about as though it's your last time being in this house."

Chapter 10

“What are you talking about? I can't just pack and leave. I am very much attached to everything I own.” Nadine let out a little awkward laugh, “Either way, I will leave you two to talk everything out. I understand that I am the third wheel in here.”

Emilia let out a small sigh in exasperation, her voice wry. “Forget it. You don't have to trust me. I thought she might be able to convince you otherwise, but I guess you don't trust *her* judgment of my character.”

Nadine looked away, swallowing a lump in her throat, “That's not-”

“No. That's precisely it. You are one of those people who have major trust issues, and that clouds your current judgment of Sophia's abilities.” The red-headed slid away from the bed, approaching the desk where the tray of cups still stood, “I know that better than anyone because I am that way. However, she looked around the desk, observing some of the papers scattered around, and took one of the cups in her hand, turning towards them, “You seem to be a better person than I could ever possibly be.”

Which is precisely why I need to protect you by any means.

Nadine glanced up, giving Emilia a sympathetic look, "If I am such a great person, then why do I live so much in my own imagination? Isn't that because I am afraid to face reality?"

"No. You simply refuse to accept the world the way it is right now. That is your greatest strength."

This kid is very much like a better version of me.

The petite girl's eyes widened a little, and she nodded firmly, "I can see why you won, Sophia. You read people so easily."

"You make me sound as though I am a psychic." Emilia let out a chuckle, "Look. It would be such a waste to let those teas go cold. Sophia and I were outside in a cold rain. Let's just drink them and calm down."

"I have low blood pressure. I am always calm." Nadine remarked as she accepted the tea that Emilia gave her.

"I can see why you won, Sophia as well." Emilia commented, giving her partner another cup of tea and then finally taking the last one in her own hands, "May I ask, have you put any sweeteners inside?"

"Just two cubes of sugar. One for Phia. She likes it bitter. We are out of honey, berries, and milk. Sorry." The petite girl decided to sit at the desk, shifting on her chair a little.

Emilia mumbled something along the lines of 'no worries' and decided to take a sip.

Chapter 11

Sophia stood still and just observed the scene. She remembered when they had stolen food from that small child in Africa. Even up until that day, she had still sometimes dream of that little girl and what happened to her.

The butterfly effect was terrifying.

"You stole my sister! You monster!"

Except someone stole away your dad, Nadine, my dear friend.

She glanced at the cup of tea in her hands and decided to sit on the soft bed. Closing her eyes, she found herself going over everything that had happened in that lengthy day.

Although, it's not like this was her first time having one of those days whose outcomes stretched as though they happened over the course of years and not only a mere few hours.

Moreover, what was wrong with her?

Emanuel was murdered by a robot, and then boom! Out of nowhere, Emilia was back, saving her life.

A creeping feeling of guilt washed over her due to the fact that she slapped Emilia, but she couldn't help herself. It was as though only when Nadine prompted to know more that something fuelled her anger, and instantly, she just shouted and slapped Emilia.

But...

Emilia became a part of her, and even if she wished she didn't need her, the reality was different.

Brutal honestly and borderline gray morality was something that Emilia excelled at, and it's what fuelled Sophia to be stronger because—

Because she couldn't let Emilia do all the work.

Because Emilia would have her back no matter what.

Because had she murdered someone, Emilia wouldn't question it but would help her to hide the body.

Because Emilia understood her deepest desires without asking.

Because...she wanted to impress Emilia.

Because when she showed up in pieces, Emilia made her whole.

I can think of a thousand and one because...

But only one was enough.

Because it's you, Em.

"I am here. It's going to be alright." She suddenly heard, which pulled her out of her train of thought, and she looked over to the speaker.

Emilia offered her a small smile that was so-like-her, and Sophia found herself bashful, no words coming out of her mouth. Only her partner could say the words she needed to hear, so she nodded.

"I know...I know because it's you."

And with that statement, a warm and long-forgotten smile made its way on Sophia's face in Emilia's direction, "Shit, woman, do you have any idea how much I have missed you."

Nadine hid her smirk and pretended not to pay attention to both of them, secretly shedding tears of joy.

Chapter 12

They drank the tea in comfortable silence, each girl drowning in her own inner sea of countless questions.

Emilia glanced at the clock that was on the wall.

A few more minutes.

Her thoughts were confirmed when Nadine started yawning, rubbing her eyes a little, "This is weird."

Sophia raised an eyebrow at her, "What precisely?"

"I know my body more than the average human does know about their own. This sudden fatigue? Sleepiness? I dunno…It's not *usual* shit. Feels like anesthesia."

Emilia stayed silent, observing the duo.

"That's impossible. You didn't take anything out of the ordinary, right?" the brunette decided to approach Nadine, who was now leaning heavily on the table, shaking her head in confirmation that she followed her usual routine, "Nadine!"

The petite girl lowered her head even more but didn't respond. Sophia shook her a little in fear and confusion, "Nadine!"

"Don't." Emilia took one of Sophia's hands, "She is fine. Just asleep. For the next two hours. That should be plenty of time."

The brunette flinched a little, narrowing her eyes in confusion with a trace of anger. "You *drugged* her?! What is wrong with you?"

The red-headed smirked a little, beaming with her usual confidence, "I would like to know that myself. And yes, I did drug her, but only because there was no other way to get her to come with us without being suspicious or causing a scene."

"But..."

"But what? Would you prefer if I let her die in here?"

"There you go again. What makes you so sure she would be attacked?"

"...."

"Emilia! For fuck sake, give me one answer! I am begging you!" Sophia raised her voice, clutching her hands in anticipation, "Just one."

"If I were to tell you right now, I would need to drug you *too*." Emilia let out a sigh, "Just...*trust* me. I am trying my damn best to save her. Pack her stuff, and let's get the fuck out of here."

"She is going to hate me if I help you now." Sophia swallowed a lump in her throat, looking around, "Is there any way to pack her whole house. Heh...like she said, she is very much attached to her stuff."

Emilia let out a huge sigh in annoyance, "No, but I will find a way. In fact, I already have an idea. Just pack the essentials for now." She made her way to the window, placing one of her hands on the glass, murmuring, "After everything I thought I lost before...."

"What?" the brunette asked from the other side of the room, quickly packing some clothes, papers, medications, and other stuff that she deemed were the essential part of Nadine's belongings.

This little idiot will always make sense of everything.

The mere fact that I laughed at her view of the world shows that, perhaps, I might be the biggest idiot out of everyone.

"Just be a good girl, and do as I say without any questions."

"*No.*" Sophia raised her voice a little, still packing Nadine's stuff. "I refuse to do that. At least answer one fucking question. You think it's meaningless, but to me, it's everything I have right now."

The red-headed girl immediately turned around, approaching Sophia, who was picking some stuff from the closet and placing everything in a big coffer, "Don't ever assume that it means nothing to me, you *idiot.*" Emilia slammed her fist on the closet, her voice having a clear edge to them as though they were interchangeably wrapped with warmth and venom, "I will answer all of your questions later, I promise. But right now, one of us needs to be in their right state of mind."

Sophia didn't even flinch at her reaction but moved her gaze to her partner, smiling bitterly, "Bold of you to assume that I was ever in the right state of mind since you left."

"I wish I was there," Emilia replied without thinking, her eyes softening a little.

The brunette narrowed her eyes in confusion, "What?"

"I wish I was there with you. But shit happened. After some time, I lost myself. If anything, life was certainly not spoiling you either." She shook her head a little, not sure what she was trying to say, "If anything, I am still chasing some resemblance of happiness, so my little idiot, say you will come with me this time?"

Sophia teared up a little, her face grimacing, and without warning, she tightly hugged Emilia, who stood there in shock, "Till the end, Em. Till the end. And even if years pass by, the apple that you, *we-* were chasing is still out there. I only wish for us to find that happiness once again."

Emilia returned her embrace, closing her eyes. "You grew so strong...Surely, we will find it. This is the worst. It can only be better."

"No matter how long it takes."

Chapter 13

What on earth happened?

Nadine groaned a little, slowly opening and closing her eyes, not sure whether she should just go back to sleeping or wake up.

"Are you awake?" she heard a familiar voice, and she immediately felt at peace, knowing it was Sophia. Everything was fine.

But it did not feel like it.

She rubbed her eyes a little and realized that this was not her bed or her room. She sat up on the bed, looking around. It was a small, bland white-grayish room with a window that was so tiny in the corner of the ceiling that you might even miss it. She hated the white light that was on the ceiling; it was giving her creeps and anxiety ticks. There was an old-

More like an ancient closet, as well as the desk and chair. No wonder the bed felt like shit.

She started shaking her right leg a little, and her sleepiness started washing away.

She noticed that Sophia was not in the same clothes as before, and her expression was clearly that of guilt. Nadine could not possibly phantom why but she decided to ignore that and focus on her location.

"Yeah..." she let out a big yawn, sleepiness still clouding her judgment, "Where are we?"

"A bunker. One of Emilia's hideouts."

"Why on earth does she needs a hideout? Is Em some sort of criminal?"

"*No!*" Sophia immediately took a defensive stance and quickly gathered her thoughts, "She is protecting us."

"From what?" Nadine raised her eyebrows, confused, "We were just chilling, and now we are hiding in a bunker? On top of that, why did she make me feel asleep?"

"What?" Sophia's eyes widened, but the petite girl noticed that her friend did not deny it, "How did you..?"

"That's the only explanation. Besides, she does..." let out a little sigh, making herself comfortable in the bed, leaning up a little, "seem to be a kind of a person who doesn't take a no for an answer."

Sophia's silence was more than enough of a confirmation, "I am sorry-"

"Don't be. Whether you were aware she would drug me doesn't matter."

"It's not just that..." Sophia scowled and buried her face in her hands, "I have no idea how to tell you this."

"I am a big girl. I can endure everything." Nadine smiled a little, hiding her worry for Sophia.

"Even big girls can get hurt." The brunette showed her face once again as though she was recalling something.

"Just say it."

Taking a deep sigh as though she was mentally preparing herself for another mental battle (not that she needed any additional ones), Sophia briefly explained the events of everything that had happened at the graveyard, and Emanuel hearing a noise-

"And then he pushed me to the wet grass, and when I looked up, he...was shot...by a robot. Something that resembles those AIs that were banned in the past. Next thing I know, Emilia destroyed that robot, and...you know the rest." The brunette finished, and slowly her eyes went up, realizing that Nadine was oddly silent, and her gaze looked lost, seemingly staring right at Sophia.

Dad...is dead.

My dad is dead...No.

No. No. No. No!!!

He was killed!

"Who?" Nadine whispered, all of the emotions mixing into anger, fuelling rage of an extent that seemed out of this world for her; ignoring the river of tears on her face, she repeated, "Who?"

"Who, what?"

"Who sent that robot?" she asked as though she was asking for a receipt, her gaze still on the same place, "Who *the fuck* sent that robot?"

She was proud to say that there were only a handful of moments when she cursed in her life; however, at that moment, it was as though the reality was too real, and nothing but rage was leading her.

She clutched her hands, her body shaking a little as she shouted, "Answer me!"

"I don't know! Nadine, sweety, please, I understand how you feel, but-"

"You understand nothing! Your mother died due to illness whilst the only family member I *had* left was murdered by an old piece of trash!"

Sophia ignored that comment about her mother and focused on the fact that Nadine was emotionally suffering and that, frankly, her reaction to the murder of her parent was way too familiar, and she was more than aware that that bloody road leads to nothing but misery and despair.

"Does she know? What happened to his body? I just...want answers so badly! Nothing is making any sense." Nadine clutched her knees to her chest, crying, sobbing, and hurting on every level.

Sophia decided to sit still. She felt as though she wasn't inclined to be the one to comfort Nadine.

Chapter 14

"So, let me get this straight. In three days, we will move to one of the, if not the most isolated island in the world?"

"Yes." Emilia said, as a matter of fact, smiling slightly, "To be honest, I am quite looking forward to it."

"You are nuts." Her brother sighed, rubbing his forehead in desperation. Sometimes, Emilia's impulsivity was really concerning.

"I know."

"Do *they* even know about this?"

"Not at the moment. I was planning on telling Sophia tomorrow." She smiled, closing her eyes, "You know, I really don't want to force you, but for your own safety, please do come with me without asking questions. Truth be told, it's inevitable at this point."

Richard's eyes furrowed in confusion at both what his sister was saying and her expression. It was a genuinely happy expression, but her voice was telling him otherwise. "What's inevitable?"

"You will see."

He rolled his eyes. He knew he would be getting an answer either way. No one could ever get the brutal answer out of Emilia ever since-

Well, ever since she became this.

This evil mastermind with her own little secret organization, always on the run, doing-

It was probably for the best he didn't know the details. All he truly needed to know was that Emilia would always be his big sister, always keeping him safe.

And he would gladly allow it because, for sure, he was too weak to stand on his own two feet after the incident that turned both of their lives upside down.

Two days passed without them doing anything in particular. Emilia went on her usual routine of playing with the world without telling anyone, whilst Sophia would be silently reading a book in her room without bothering anyone and only talking to Richard here and there.

Nadine, despite her life literally being thrown into the abyss and her world shattered out of nowhere, was acting rather...*normal.*

It was as though she transferred her whole life in that small room inside the bunker, obeying perfectly everything that Sophia would require of her, which wasn't anything out of the ordinary. She would eat and take her medications when required. Hell, she even asked for sweets after lunch on the two days. And when she wasn't doing the basic stuff that humans need, she would write.

Write as though she was running out of time, write as though that was the only thing that kept her alive. The only thing she requested from Sophia was to ask Emilia for more paper.

Emilia didn't think of it too much, for she didn't know the girl that well. She did, however, come to the conclusion that misery was inspiring.

After all, weren't all the best creators a little messed up? Aren't all the best characters just beautifully incorporated whilst they were walking on a thin line of gray morality?

And just like always, Emilia had trouble falling asleep (what a shocker), so she decided not to chug down a bottle of sleeping pills but a rather gentle approach like a glass of milk. She remembered the time when she had trouble falling asleep years ago at Sophia's place, and her little partner would explain to her that a glass of milk was welcomed because it contained a good amount of sweet melatonin.

She made her way to the kitchen and realized that the milk was already on the table and that she was not alone at such a late hour.

"Oh? Trouble falling asleep?" she asked, taking a mug with stars in her hands and sitting across from the petite girl. She poured some milk inside the mug, giving her a half-assed smile.

"No, actually- I was writing. I just got a little hungry, that's all." Nadine replied, playing with her bowl of cereal a little. It didn't seem as though there were many left; she must have been hungry.

"You do realize that writing is not going to run away? You should take care of your body first and then finish that story of yours. It's two in the morning." Emilia said in a motherly tone, taking a sip, "If anyone understands ambition, then it's me."

"I don't think you understand. I wouldn't be able to fall asleep if I kept it inside my head. Writers are not the master of the words; it's quite the opposite, actually." She chuckled a little and placed the spoon inside her mouth, some of the cereals sliding off the spoon back into the bowl.

The older girl narrowed her eyes in confusion. "I thought you are right-handed," looking at Nadine in curiosity as she kept eating.

A pitiful smile crossed the smaller girl's face, and she nodded. "MS attack. It will pass....hopefully." She whispered the last word but underestimated that Emilia had perfect hearing.

The red-headed girl averted her gaze in confusion. "Should I wake up Sophia? This is her field. I don't understand your conditions that much."

Nadine shook her head, hiding her emotional and physical misery behind another joke, taking her spoon in her right hand, which made her feel look like a toddler who didn't know how to hold a spoon.

"It feels as though my muscles have a tight band-aid around them, making me...well, I am not able to use and control my body properly. Parts of them, that is. I am fine...I *live* on."

"I am sorry to hear that," Emilia replied, which made the smaller girl glare at her as though she had just insulted her ancestors.

"Do *not* be. I despise pity. That's just how things are."

Nodding, Emilia decided to drop the subject. She herself hated pity more than anything.

"No need to force a smile in front of me." Em said, "We can talk openly about everything."

"Well, excuse me, your highness. I have literally *nothing*, including control over my body, so I am sorry for trying to cope with everything the best I can!" Nadine snapped, clutching her fists, tears appearing in the corner of her eyes. "I barely know you. I don't even want to talk with Sophia about it, let alone you! Daniel was right. The only reason I can live on is because I live in my imagination. At least I could do that while my dad was alive. I don't need to talk with anyone about anything. Just leave me be. I will live on."

Em said nothing.

The pain of being a part of nothingness itself was deadly familiar to her.

And so, just like her partner, Emilia decided to sit still. She felt as though she wasn't inclined to be the one to comfort Nadine.

Chapter 15

Something is very wrong.

At first, I thought it would be...my lifestyle but-

Emilia helplessly looked at her left hand, which made an involuntary movement.

I can deny it no longer.

This is a sign of...something.

For a moment, she smiled at herself in pity, but even she couldn't deny the anxiety building up inside her, swallowing her whole, her heart beating faster, her ears ringing, and suddenly her world became very small and limited to her own room.

Breath!

Just breath!

"It's nothing. I am overthinking this. All is well. All is well. All is well..." she kept repeating to herself like a mantra; more specifically, the one she didn't believe herself.

But what possibly could she do?

Asking for help or telling anyone about this was out of the question.

Suddenly she snapped out of the anxiety attack by slamming her hand hard against the wall.

The sudden pain in her knuckles made her feel in control again, and she ignored the bangs that fell over her eyes, staring into the small blood sliding down her hand. Her hand was bruised, but it did not matter.

She did not matter.

She just had to continue on.

She had so much to do.

Health was her second priority.

It *had to* be.

The knock on her door startled her for a moment, but she quickly snapped out of her thoughts and hid her hands in the pocket of her hoodie, inviting the person in.

The familiar brunette let herself inside, and immediately Emilia offered her a small smile, "What brings you here?"

Sophia fixed her hair a little, still staring right into Emilia's eyes, "Why?"

"Why what?" Emilia raised her eyebrows.

Her partner made a 'tch' sound and shook her head, "You know damn well what I am talking about. Your brother told me we are leaving this evening..." she narrowed her eyes in confusion with a trace of anger in her voice as though she was speaking about something unbelievable which wasn't too far from the truth "To a remote island?"

"Oh, that. Yeah." Emilia shrugged her shoulders, "What's the issue?"

"Gee, I don't know. Maybe the fact that you could have, at least, informed us about it. I.." Sophia clutched her hands, "I understand that you probably don't care about my or Nadine's thoughts on the matter. After all...we are clueless about everything. The two of us are useless to you."

No, you little idiot.

It's me who is going to quite useless if my body doesn't snap out of this shit.

Emilia moved her gaze from Sophia in a bit of guilt, ignoring the ever-familiar trace of longing, "It never fails to amaze me that someone like you think so lowly of herself."

"What do you mean by that?"

"Never mind it. I know you are not an egotistical bitch like me." Emilia smirked a little, looking longingly at Sophia, "That's one of the things I like about you."

The brunette snuffled on her foot, and Emilia assumed that her little partner was probably going over that statement. Sophia opened her mouth, but no words came out.

Finally, she spoke, laughing in between with a trace of bitterness, "You always do this."

"Do what?" she asked, sitting down on the bed, still keeping her hands in her pockets.

"Throwing me off balance. I came to this room with a solid argument and a damn good reason to be mad at you, and then you...do this. Say things like *that*." Sophia raised her hands up in the air a little, gesturing her emotions as though she was holding a speech, "You always take control of everything."

Ha!

My sweet little idiot had you only known the extent of the control you had over me.

The red-headed was silent for a moment, just smiling a little, albeit more to herself than Sophia. She stood up even though she had sat down a second ago, walking confidently towards Sophia, whose confusion and sweet anxiety were very much visible in her brown poles.

"And yet, you never complain. You always let me take care of everything." She stood right in front of Sophia, staring right into her eyes, her voice lowering a little, "Ever since day one."

She bit her lip a little, playing with her hands, "I...of course, I would. It's *you*. I know you. Sometimes you are even so brutally honest that I wish you would lie."

"Lie to you? I am not going to do that. I might be a monster, but at least I am not lying. Not to *you*, at least."

"You are *not* a monster, Em."

"You have no idea what I have done. And... have been doing." Emilia started playing with a few strands of Sophia's soft hair.

"Yes...but it's you. You could burn the whole world, and I would still find a reason to keep trusting you."

"You put too much faith into me." She tucked the strands of her partner's hair behind her ear, smiling a little.

"Or you put too little faith in yourself."

Nah, I just know myself a little too much.

"Perhaps...that's why you make me whole."

Chapter 16

Sophia always took pride in the fact that despite her life being a complete and utter mess, she remained stable in every sense of the word.

No matter what, her mind would always reset itself back to its original stability, no matter the circumstances.

Perhaps she really did give herself too little credit.

But then again, she was never as proud full as Emilia.

When Emilia started playing with the strands of her own long brown hair, she didn't let herself be excited. It would be so stupid and nonsensical.

"Perhaps...that's why you make me whole."

At that moment, she had to remind herself that she was a grown-ass woman, almost in her 40s.

She was not supposed to let her loneliness kick in at the sound of her voice or sight.

She was not supposed to be led by pure emotions and ignore her rationality.

And yet, there she was, still feeling like a teenager every single time when Emilia decided to be Emilia.

Her heart skipped a few times, and despite not being religious, she prayed that the woman before her did not hear it.

Then...just like that night...

What's stopping you in this life?

"Em..." she barely whispered her name, trying her best to analyze the woman that stood before her but just as always, she would remain a mystery, her emotions completely clouded in those cold but rather soft green wonderlands.

"You deserve better," Emilia said whilst taking a step back and then making her way out of the room.

You, too.

Sophia's breath hitched, and she stood on the spot motionless. As she slowly started getting back to her senses, she felt nostalgic for anything that might have been but decided that mourning over it was not going to ease any of her pain.

In reality, there were way too many sources of suffering that affected her, and the main issue was her own helplessness to change anything.

She decided to seize the opportunity that she was alone in Emilia's bedroom. For a moment, she felt conflicted over going through any of her stuff by remembering how it ended up last time with Daniel but-

No matter how wicked Emilia was, she was not nearly as fucked up as Daniel was.

Which reminded her she really needed to tell Emilia about him. Or perhaps, Emilia already knew? She couldn't forget the fact that Emilia knew exactly where to find her and save her with a very convenient pistol.

She also had a connection to Emanuel.

Her partner had promised to tell her anything but so far, getting any answer out of her led to "I am too busy" and "Talk to ya later.".

Her brother was not well informed either.

She looked around the small room, which was very much similar to the ones that she and Nadine had.

A bed with a comfortable-looking mattress, an old-looking night table with a lamp, and a desk with a laptop that didn't look similar to a regular one; at least, she didn't see the name of the brand. She thought it might be a good source, but knowing Emilia, it had a password or some sort of protection.

She decided to approach a small bookshelf and noticed that it was filled with various genres of books from many different authors, including some of the Russian and English classics. She recognized most of them, and she also noticed that Emilia was a very well of manga collector like Nadine.

She remembered a huge collection that Nadine possessed in her room in her home.

Sophia glanced around the room one time and decided to take a seat on the bed.

Perhaps she wasn't destined to find anything, and-

"Ooof!" she grimaced as soon as she made contact with the bed. Despite the mattress looking extremely comfortable, her bottom still felt as though she sat on some tough material.

Instinctively, she moved away to the softer part of the mattress and decided to take a look at what she had just sat on.

Moving the pillow away a little bit, Sophia realized it was a notebook, a fluffy and cute-looking one as well.

She thought that it was kind of bizarre that someone like Emilia had a notebook like that in their possession.

Curiosity took the best of her, and soon she realized by the handwriting as well as the content that this was Emilia's diary.

But why?

Why would Emilia have it in such a place?

It wasn't even under the locket.

It was so easy to find it and open it.

Although...Emilia never liked to share a room, and I don't think that Rocky would go in her bedroom in the first place. He trusts Emilia unconditionally.

*I do too...It's just that I **know** her.*

She can so easily get lost in her own mind, and she already went through such a mess.

I need to know the whole truth.

With that, she cursed that she didn't get her phone with her, so she quickly found a random book to replace it underneath Emilia's pillow and snuck away into her own room to read Emilia's diary.

Here goes nothing.

Chapter 17

If I don't write down my thoughts, I am going to go crazy. Not that I was ever sane in the first place.

Ah, diary, diary, diary

Where should I start?

Perhaps with how I escaped? Or how come I was a suspect in the first place? Who is the real Demon? Where is he now?

"He..." Sophia whispered to herself, swallowing a lump; she would lie if she said she wasn't a little shaken by it. So many years ago, her life took such a drastic turn due to this demon, and she never even got a full explanation of who exactly *he* was nor what *his* goal was.

Heck, until a second ago, she didn't even know the gender of this person.

You see, my diary, in order for my story to be written, I shall start from the beginning. It all started with a man called Andreas Walter.

"Hold the fuck up...Andreas Walter...."

....Daniel and Lilly Schneider...product of human darkness...and as a matter of fact, they were not meant to be your average people.

Perfect world....4th Reich....They were merely the products...and ultimately victims by design.

Sophia clutched her fists, skimming through the pages that contained the information that she already knew about from Daniel *himself*. From the *Demon* himself as well as his diary.

And my dear diary, you want to know how I know this?

The Demon himself told me.

And I understood him. I just didn't care.

But in the end, I just could not kill him. I didn't just see him. I saw a devastatingly broken boy that was merely a few years older than my own little brother. I simply couldn't. I killed before. I killed his accomplices, at least the ones that were involved in my parents' murder, and took everything that I possibly could.

However, I couldn't destroy him. There was no need.

His mere existence was already enough of a punishment.

And that was enough to cover the wound that sought revenge as clarity.

"Bloody hell..." Sophia closed the diary for a moment, her hand running through her hair, taking in deep breaths. That was a twist she did not expect.

She was still very much processing what she had just read.

If Emilia was aware of Daniel's true nature, then why would she let Sophia be involved with him in any way?

Part of her felt the relief that she always wished for; because, finally, she had closure of everything that happened with the Demon. She finally knew his identity, and she remembered everything that Emilia had told her about his motives.

She never doubted that her partner was not correct. Reading people's true nature was something that was Emilia's second nature. That is, right after being a bitch to the world.

Another thought crossed her mind as well.

This Emilia had committed a murder. No, correction. Murders.

But I still cannot call her a murderer. She didn't kill for fun.

She...was broken. She just...used the power she had in her hands to get the revenge that she so deeply wanted.

And I can't object to that. It's not my place. Not my pain and not my story. Which is, ultimately, why I can't object to her actions.

I just hope that at the end of the day, she doesn't regret it.

But...

She certainly is not happy.

Sophia still did not fully understand Emilia's full involvement with Daniel, but one way or another, she was bound to find it. Whether through the diary or Emilia herself.

However, remembering the despair that she saw in Emilia's eyes, she...

Hearing a knock on the door and Emilia's familiar voice, she quickly shut the diary, pushed it under the closet, and approached the door.

I need to get Em out of her own pretty little head.

"I brought you your favorite tea. Bitter with just a hint of sweetness, just like you prefer."

Sophia opened the door, looking surprised at the beautiful-looking cup with, nonetheless, her favorite brand of chamomile tea. She felt incredibly touched by this little gesture, not caring that it was still a rather weak attempt on Emilia's side to reconcile the fact that she had not told them about moving away without even as much as informing them.

She smiled longingly, taking the small tray in her hands.

But it was Em. And ultimately, it did not matter.

She would always let it slide.

After all, she would rather have her by her side in some way than not having her in her life at all.

Chapter 18

"So, only 15 hours, and we are going to be on the other side of the world." Nadine looked with a blank stare in her eyes, her voice, however, not fitting her out-of-this-world stare.

"Yes, Tristan da Cunha, here we go." The man said with a weird dose of enthusiasm, "Out of all the places that we visited, this is the one I am honestly looking forward to."

Sophia looked around the shipyard, small but dark fog surrounding them. Truth be told, she wasn't even particularly sure of that exact shipyard they were at, but she found herself not really caring about such trivial detail. She trusted Emilia. She also knew very well from the experience that Emilia was more than capable of getting them alive and well to their destination.

And so, they got inside a submarine, only their personal stuff with them; she didn't question anything.

All she knew was that their belongings, such as clothes and other things that people possess, were already...well...at the island.

She had some small questions, mostly to satisfy her own curiosity, but overall, she didn't question anything that Emilia did.

After all, Emilia was a woman who kept both of them alive during their own journey as well. She literally brought them back to Germany from the other side of the world and kept up with the world no matter the situation.

Sophia wasn't capable of any of that. She was very well aware of that. Cold rationality that required actions was not her strongest suit.

Emilia showed Nadine her cabin inside, which she happened to share with Sophia. Richard had a comfy-looking mattress in the main area that was not particularly big but still not claustrophobic either. The walls consisted mainly of incredibly thick glass, which Sophia greatly appreciated.

"What about you, though?" Sophia asked, looking at Emilia in concern. She was no fool to the fact that her partner did not rock the dark eye bags because they were trendy. They were not as notable since Emilia had glasses, but she still noticed them.

"The chair in the control room looks good." Her partner brushed it off, staring into the deep blue ocean, admiring the corals and fish as well as the occasional jellyfish that she noticed, "Everything is already programmed, but I don't trust auto-pilots enough to fall asleep."

"Then I am going to keep you company." Sophia immediately replied, smiling warmly.

Emilia shook her head a little, disinterested. "There is no need to. In fact, I would prefer to be alone."

Oh.

That hurts.

Sophia ignored the spreading pain that Emilia caused and gave a small nod.

Noticing that Richard and Nadine were in the other room, Emilia stepped in front of Sophia with an apologizing smile on her face, "Phia, you know better than anyone else; it's nothing personal.

After all, you are one of the very few people I *want* to tolerate. It's just that...I have been alone for so long, and I have come to the realization that solitude is more addictive than drugs."

"I know." Sophia let out a deep sigh, biting her lip a little, lowering her gaze a little at nothing in particular, "But I also know that it can mess up anyone if consumed a little too much."

"Bold of you to assume that I haven't been messed up in the first place." The red-haired woman chuckled a little, which for a second sounded a little maniacal, but Sophia didn't think anything of it. Her voice lowered a little, and she added, "If only you knew...."

The brunette, out of habit, put both of her hands in her pockets out of anxiety that danced inside her. Emilia knew.

Emilia fucking *knew* that she had her diary. She was mocking her purely for her own amusement.

However, she wanted to step up her game and show off to Emilia that she was very much capable of playing this game as well.

After all, she played it really well with Daniel for some time, so dealing with her old partner was not even on the same level. It was more like the first level that she had passed a long time ago.

And perhaps, to impress her as well. To show off that she was not that naïve little girl from more than a decade ago.

"What makes you think I don't know everything?" Sophia replied as she looked up at Emilia's wonderlands.

Emilia studied her little partner for a moment under intense gaze before replying with a smirk on her face, "Because you would not be here. Because, by some miracle, if you stayed, you would be lecturing me on morals and that I should not be playing a goddess."

"Maybe I just learned a long time ago that it's impossible to change your mind when you set your mind on something."

"Nah, it's you we are talking about. You were always able to see the good in people. To stop people when needed. To sympathize in this cruel world. That, and you would be losing your mind about the future." She replied with a certain amount of grief in her voice, looking away, "But I don't care. After all, I owe you an explanation. I don't give a fuck about the world, but I do give a few for you. Which is why I am doing what I am doing. You will find out about everything if you continue reading."

And, like always, you are spot on.

"But...I would rather hear it from you. I read bits here and there, but just more and more questions keep pilling up."

"Read everything, and then I will answer all of the questions you have. But I gotta warn you." Emilia turned away, walking towards the control room, "Once you know everything, you will have to stay with me. I don't have it in me to silence you."

"Yeah, that answer will surely help me to fall asleep."

"*Tibia* honest, I am kinda looking forward to it. After all, you are a very *patient* person." With that, Emilia left the main room, and after the realization hit Sophia's head, she burst out laughing, which was something that she hadn't done in quite a while.

Oh, Em, you perfect bitch.

Chapter 19

Emilia sat on the small mattress in the control room, observing the screen that was showing their location as well as the coordinates that they were following.

The room was rather small but very comfortable for one person.

She smiled bitterly for a second. As though she deserved anything better. All of the money she possessed was stolen from greedy bastards that would not even notice a couple of hundreds missing or through other illegal means. Some of it was even from that man that they found ages ago on the boat, which Sophia would find out soon. She did not even want to remember the fact that the majority of "her" money was originally Daniel's.

Which, in the end, means that all of her money was covered in blood in one way or another.

She thought back at the fact that soon enough, Sophia was going to find out everything.

Ah, my dearest idiot, did you seriously think I wouldn't know?

...

After all, even now, after all of this time, I am still searching for that one thing.

Perhaps...you have been the key the whole time.

No, maybe I have always known that you are the key to my apple. I just thought that if I lied enough, eventually, I would deceive myself as well.

But that's not how it works, right?

Despite me saying goodbye and trying to give you a better life from the shadows, fate brought us together even though that same fucking fate has torn away so many lives.

Ha! Some fair fate is it.

"Nah, fuck fate; it's an excuse for those who don't have control over their lives," Emilia whispered to herself, realizing that she had a whole argument with herself in her own mind.

Boredom really brings out the weirdest in humans.

Looking at the time, she realized that it was almost three in the morning. Well, night.

"Who the hell wakes up at 3am in their right mind? Unless they have a night shift, I just can't imagine anyone doing that voluntarily."

Once again, she thought back at how much Sophia could possibly read by that time.

Chances were that she already knew about Daniel. That the real Demon of their time was Daniel. That that was purely one of his many roles.

That in a way, when she realized that ultimately she could not kill him, she not only used *him* as one of her pawns but also saved him as well.

The moment when she, a pawn in his game, overthrew the God, or more precisely, the Demon, the supposedly next Hitler, and took away everything that he had.

The moment when she caught up with the Demon's plan and actually became the Demon herself.

The video in which I lied to you that everything was according to my plan...

But at the end of the day, does it matter who started everything?

It became my own game.

"I became everything that I despised. And yet, I still think I am better than everyone." Emilia closed her eyes for a moment, letting out a yawn.

At this point, Sophia probably knew that in the end, Emilia herself saved Daniel by taking his role and making him her pawn and that he didn't care about anything other than staying alive as long as he wasn't found by the police.

That Ronald, his right-hand man, was the one who planted the fake evidence, which was why Emilia was suspected to be the Demon way before she was a Demon in reality. And he was the man who executed her parents and ended up being executed by her; her very first murder.

And, oh, how could she possibly forget her perfect plan of deceiving the Demon.

She grinned to herself, thinking of the time she spent at the court, laughing and talking nonsense until she fooled everyone.

Smile, smile.

Laugh, laugh.

And you will fool the world.

After all, it was easier to get away from a mental institution than it would be from prison. Perhaps the time she had spent at the University wasn't in vain after all.

Ah, statistics.

Who knew you would give me that crazy idea.

Abruptly, she heard the door opening, and she averted her gaze to the door noticing none other than her little idiot with a small smile on her face. Opening the door, she went inside with two cups of something.

"I thought I might join you." Sophia slid down on the mattress next to her after she placed both of the cups on the tiny table that was in front of them.

"If you find watching an arrow and numbers fun, then I am certainly not the weird one in this room."

Letting out a chuckle, Sophia took the cup that was in front of her, enjoying the warm sensation from the cup.

A small silence settled upon them as they both sat there as though unsure how to go over everything they both knew. There was so much to unpack, and none of them knew where to start or how to address anything.

Until Sophia decided to break that silence. "Thank you."

"What for?"

"I am on that part in your diary where you wrote that you decided to give the fairest treatment of the world you possibly could. Meaning that my job...you were the one responsible for the boss even hiring me in the first place. You even remembered my dream place."

"Oh, that. No need for thanking me." Emilia ignored the beating of her own heart and smiled warmly at Sophia, "Really."

Out of the blue, Sophia leaned her head on her partner's shoulder, staring into nothing in particular, "Remember the time we spent in Africa? Our journey after we were kidnapped?"

At that moment, Emilia was hyper-aware of Sophia's emotional proximity, and her first instinct was to push her away, but something else stopped her, and she just hummed in response.

"I didn't understand so much, and I still don't, but...at times, it felt like it was only us in the whole wide world. Everything else was just there. And...I regretted. Regretted not being braver and stopping you from leaving."

Emilia's heart skipped a beat, and her lips trembled for a moment, just a tiny bit, "I regret not being selfish the only time it mattered."

Sophia moved her head away, sitting next to her in silence.

Okay, I did not plan to say that aloud-

Out of the blue, her little idiot cupped her cheeks, her hands still warm from the cup, as the lights from the screen bathed them.

"Please, tell me you are not joking with me. Because if you do, then you are truly the cruelest." Sophia spoke, her brown poles tearing up from what she assumed was a mix of everything.

Emilia sat still, smiling as she gave Sophia a smile that she had thought was so lost and forgotten. Then, she gently placed a hand on her partner's mouth, leaving a peck on her own hand that was burning with Sophia's scent.

She moved away her head, placing her index finger on her own mouth, winking at the shocked and embraced brunette that was still gasping a little. She didn't need to try hard to be able to read Sophia's exhilaration spiced with bashfulness.

"Maybe in another world, there was no barrier between us." The red-headed woman spoke in a hushed tone as she took her own cup.

Sophia gathered her thoughts and composure as much as she could, her emotions still wild and overwhelming from Emilia's action, "Why is there one in the first place?"

The red-headed woman smiled bitterly, closing her eyes, "Because it is too late for me to find happiness in this life. So maybe in another lifetime, both of us would be a little braver."

And because you could never possibly be with someone like me after you know the whole truth.

"Let me guess, I will get the answers once I finish reading the diary."

"In a way...."

Sophia lowered her gaze, silent.

.

.

.

"Damn you, you gorgeous bitch." The brunette spoke confidently, which made Emilia look at her with surprise and intrigue in her eyes, "You really do just whatever the fuck you want without thinking of the impact that you have on others even after all those years?"

The red-headed smirked a little, narrowing her eyes a tiny bit at Sophia, "My sweet little idiot, that's the smallest sin I have committed in all those years."

Sophia shook her head a little, thoughts running through her mind, "Still with that nickname?"

"Of course, it's *yours*."

The brunette let out a strained chuckle, "At least it's better than all those medical puns you used to make."

Emilia raised her hand, making a weird gesture, "They were fabulous, and you know it."

"I got one question, though."

"Shoot."

"Where is your dog? I have seen it in the city. Or am I just not on that part in your diary?"

"What are you talking about? I never had a dog." Emilia narrowed her eyebrows in confusion.

"But...I saw it when I was out around the time I met Daniel. *Uhuru* was its name. It's just that...what are the odds of someone naming a dog when we had talked about it. The name is so specific." Sophia explained.

"Yeah, we talked about it in Africa, but Phia, I never had a dog."

Sophia narrowed her eyes in confusion, "That's...not possible. I swear I saw it! Ohhh, I know. You are just screwing me with me."

No, I am not.

What the hell is wrong with you? Have you started doing some drugs?

Are you having hallucinations?

Sophia laughed it off, but Emilia stayed silent, thinking it over. Was Sophia getting mentally ill?

However, an explosion going off in the ocean in their close proximity rudely broke their conversation.

Chapter 20

*N*o, no, no!
Please, God, universe, aliens, whatever, please, I need just a little bit of luck in this life.

Emilia swallowed the lump in her throat, her eyes wide in shock as she stared into the screen on the wall. She was holding her head since the explosion that happened nearby caused their vehicle to jolt roughly. She hit her head a bit but would survive, and she was pretty sure, at the moment, everyone in the submarine was alright.

Calm down.

I need to calm down. If I panic now, everyone dies. Everyone that I care about is on this ship.

She forced herself to take a very deep breath in and out, trying to clear her mind. What on Earth was their best course of action?

"Agh...my back. What...was that?" Sophia asked in confusion, rubbing her back, "Nevermind. I am gonna check up on Nadine and Richard." She said, leaving the room.

Approaching the screen, Emilia stared at their coordinates and the exact location of the explosion. She licked her dry lips very quickly, lowering her head a bit.

Should she press the stop button? After all, what if there were more submarines at this level just waiting for something to move?

Pressing the stop button, her hand ran through her head. Staying on that spot was certainly not a good idea. It just screamed for them to be killed.

Criminals always return to the scene of a crime.

And whoever...or whatever group did this would do it again for sure.

Somewhere in the back of her head mind, she started sliding down one of her tread of thoughts. They were in the Netherlands' sea territory, which means, if her train of thought was correct, it could be another poking at the unstable peace over the world.

First, Germany – an incident with that robot.

Secondly, Netherlands.

And a few other occasions that crossed her mind as well that happened in Austria and Belgium thus far.

Ah, politics. You seductive bitch of a monster in disguise.

That aside, it could be China, the US, or Russia. All of the countries that crossed her mind were EU members.

Wait, Balkan countries weren't left untouched either, despite them not really having the biggest influence or power overall. Considering the iron-friendship that they had with Russia (which, ethnically speaking, were mostly all Slavs, so it made sense) and China (she was unaware of details), she realized that the US pretty much fitted had all the checkmarks due to their recent political affairs as well as the military technology.

Either way, it didn't matter. This attack was just one of many over the world that recently happened.

She stared at the two big buttons in front of her. This was, by far, one of the most important times in her life where she wished she didn't always have to bear the burden of having to actually decide about something as big.

Usually, she relished in the throne of power and decision-making, consumed by her own greed for more.

But knowing that this one decision, which would ultimately be decided by luck, could result in the death of all of the people she cared for was too much.

Her right hand shook as she eyed the two buttons in front of her. The green one would stop the auto-pilot, and they would just stand there, which might make enemies think that they were not a threat and leave.

Or just kill all of us without us even trying to save our lives.

The red button was not any more seductive. It would make them move very fast, which might make their enemy think they were running away because they were hurt.

Or just send another explosion right at us coz they are probably closer to us now.

The worst part was that she didn't even have time to sit down and think through any of it. Another explosion might come any minute.

She had to decide.

She had to decide *quickly.*

"We have higher chances of surviving the Russian roulette." She murmured in anger, staring at the other screen, looking at what weapons their submarine had. Sliding through the list, she didn't find anything too powerful or useful until-

"Under-water fog?" she quickly read through the description of it, an idea forming in her mind.

It was a very much self-explanatory and simple principle. Additional engines would turn on at a fast speed without moving

the submarine, as well as the special liquid, which would cause an illusion of underwater fog, making the submarine "invisible" due to the density of the combo.

She licked her dry lips, looking at the other screen. It certainly would do the trick and give them enough time to get away. But how would they get away? She didn't know how fast the submarine that attacked them was fast, and she had to presume it was faster than theirs.

What if we get super close to the shore? We certainly would be less visible, and anyone seeing us close to the shore would just assume we are some amateurs or tourists.

It was their only chance.

Reluctantly, Emilia closed her eyes, saying a little prayer to herself despite not being religious, and pressed the main buttons for the fog. She immediately heard the engine as well as felt the submarine moving a bit. Her eyes trailed to the speed option, and her hand trembled for a tiny second before accelerating to the point where the red *'Alert!'* appeared before her.

She turned off the autopilot and started moving, piloting the submarine on her own.

So much for robots taking the high-pressure tasks.

"Door one locked," she ordered and ignored everyone on the other side of the door. They were alive and well, and that was all that mattered.

Following the map, she maneuvered the submarine with everything she had, not once taking a break or letting her bodily functions distract her.

She held in everything she had and completely ignored her thirst, hunger, and need for sleep, just like she had previously ignored two of the *'Alert!'* signs.

Chapter 21

T*ake me to the sea*
It's only then that my life begins.

In the end, it took them, instead of the initial 13 hours – merely 8 hours to get to their destination.

But watching the early afternoon sunlight embracing the slight waves and playing with the ocean as the summit of Queen Mary's caressed the beautiful crystal clear sky was worth it.

She ignored Sophia.

She ignored Rocky.

She ignored Nadine.

All of their frustrations with her actions or their questions did not matter.

They were safe.

She was safe.

That was all that she needed to know to allow the tears to slide down her cheeks.

Chapter 22

Once Emilia regained her composure and wiped away all of the strains of her accumulated stress and despair, she gave everyone a small smile.

"Should we go? You know, we will have to be self-sufficient on this island, so we might as well start settling down."

"H-Hold on! This is enough! You have to tell us where you plan to take us next...or anything! For God's sake, Emilia, we were attacked last night, and you completely locked in everything. When are you going to stop this?" Richard said with a stern voice, crossing his arms over his chest, "How long are we even staying in this place?"

Nadine put her hands inside her pockets, nodding. "I have to agree with Mister Wilson....First, everything with dad, and now this? What is going on?"

Sophia stayed quiet, observing Emilia's tired face, who was staring into the volcano, and observing the island from the small dock (if it even could be called one), her eyelids heavy and her expression tired. Truth be told, she had to agree with Emilia's brother and Nadine that she herself also wanted way more answers than Emilia was willing to give-

But she also knew that last night, whatever happened, Emilia possibly saved all of their lives, completely ignoring all of her needs as though she was not a physical being at all, and it was very much evident by Emilia's slightly shaking hands, body, heavy eyelids, and lethargic expression.

So, she decided to play devil's advocate and took Emilia's hand in her own, gripping them firmly, staring into her partner's eyes, "Lead the way. I can't wait to see what you have in store for us."

Thank you, Phia.

You seem to understand what I want and need when no one else does.

So, Emilia did her best to express her inner thoughts with a warm smile, gripping Sophia's hand back. With that thought, she took the role of a leader and ordered everyone to take as many things as they could, doing the same in the process.

As they followed Emilia's guide deeper into the island, they did not speak much. Rather, listening to the soft crunching of the rocks underneath their feet felt relaxing and was bringing relaxation to their worn-out minds and bodies.

As they were getting closer to the populated part of the island, they heard some voices here and there, but it was not that lively, which was normal considering the fact that it was merely dawn.

Emilia looked around, observing her surroundings a little better. She was already accustomed to the geographical position as well as the area. She had...*her* ways. She saw everything through the satellite as well as her people.

My people...

The only people that are with me but not because of the power and money are my brother and Sophia.

Everyone else...is just another pawn one way or the other.

Although, it merely bottles to the fact that I trust no body.

And no body trusts me.

All that aside, Tristan da Cunha was an interesting island. It was the most remote island in the whole world and certainly not everyone's cup of tea.

It was like time had stopped there a long time ago.

The houses were old-fashioned but not in a bad way; most of them were small one-store places that would have enough space for up to three people. Not all of them, of course. Some had a two-store or were made of different materials altogether.

The people on the island had to be self-sufficient, and due to isolation, perhaps it made sense that the time really had stopped at some point or another for them.

Despite them probably not having most of the commodities of modern life, it seemed that considering the state of the world, it was a blessing and a curse.

The island was also rich in flora and fauna for lovers of nature. The only threat that she could think of at the moment was the volcano which was very much active. However, the last time it erupted was in the 1960s, which was almost a hundred years prior to their arrival.

"Here we are." She said as they stood in the yard of a small one-store house that looked very similar to the ones they saw around. They certainly did not stand out.

One by one, they entered the house and looked around the green-white living room, which was tied to the small similar, aesthetically looking kitchen.

There were three doors inside, one of which they found out was a small bathroom with a sink, a toilet, and a bathtub.

"Who will use which room? There are two of them." Nadine asked, walking around and examining the living room as Richard opened both of the doors that led to the bedrooms, standing surprised as he opened the second room.

"Em, are you sure we are in the right place? This room seems to be occupied."

However, Sophia and Nadine noticed that the things looked rather familiar, *way too familiar,* so they decided to enter the said occupied room.

"Those are..."

"Those are my things! Everything that belonged to me is...in here?" Nadine looked bewildered and puzzled, going through her notebooks, as well as her collection of plushies and books, "But how?"

Emilia, being exhausted beyond human limits, ignored all of them, shutting down from the real world, making her way to the non-occupied room, and pushing away the big bookshelf.

Her brother, albeit puzzled, decided to help her, which soon revealed that there was a secret lock on the wall which certainly did not fit with anything that they had seen on the island so far.

Entering a six-number code, a few of the tales moved away from each other, followed by a clicking sound.

Sophia and Nadine soon stood at the entrance of the said bedroom, looking confused as well.

"Nah-ah. The last time we entered a place like that, we found that Daniel was...just no." Nadine said, shaking her hands in front of her.

"There are additional two bedrooms down there as well as the bunker room with some of my things. Nadine, you already have your things in your own room, as you requested. Richard can take this room with a secret entrance since he has the least possessions, Sophia, I hope you don't mind me choosing the room. Oh yeah, I almost forgot. There is a small Jacuzzi down there too."

They all stared at Emilia, but she ignored them and went downstairs to the said place. She flicked on the lights and was greeted by a small hallway with three brown and a bit dusty doors. She approached one of the doors and opened it as she had done it a million times, and the moment she stepped into her own bedroom, she turned on the ventilating system which thankfully happened to be extremely silent, took a deep breath in, and out, getting inside her warm and comfortable bed.

Facing her bedroom, she couldn't see a lot in the darkness. The only light that she turned on was the night table light, which didn't reflect that much of her room. She didn't have a lot in her room.

The whole room was white.

There were white walls, one wardrobe, one night table with a night lamp on it, and one bed. It was comfortable, though. It was not like she deserved something better.

However, she put her hands in front of her face a few times, noticing that her vision was not the brightest. Even without the glasses she had carefully placed on her night table, she thought to herself that her vision used to be better.

She shook it off as inhumane psychical and mental exhaustion and closed her eyes.

She really did not want to focus on her health. Knowing how bad it was and wanting to hide everything due to her own pride, she focused her mind on the things that still needed to be done.

Her mind was okay, and that was enough. It needed to be enough.

Perhaps...that attack on their submarine was one nation doing it on purpose to cause more instability in another one.

Divide and conquer has been working for humans ever since Romans.

Honestly, at this point, I don't know whether any of my plans for the perfect world have been worth anything in the grander scheme of things.

But now that I have come so far, my biggest sin would be failure.

After all, I have always possessed rage and apathy that would push me beyond mortal empathy. And then...the death of my parents just made the desire for the blood of any wrong-doer swallow this place we call home...

Perhaps only then would I drown my hatred.

Chapter 23

"Ah, you are awake."

Sometimes, I wish I didn't wake up.

. . .

No, that's for weaklings.

Emilia slowly rubbed her eyes, stretching her arms and legs, still buried deep within the blankets that warmed her very nicely. Slowly, she turned her face towards the source of the voice, only to realize that Sophia was sitting on a chair with a small bag on her lap. The red-headed did not fail to notice that her diary was now on the table as well, which could only mean one thing.

Sophia knows everything.

And yet, she still chose to be near me.

What the hell is wrong with her?

"I got us breakfast. Nothing special, just some ham sandwiches. I woke up a few hours ago, but you know me, I never had an appetite for breakfast." She chuckled a little, "Which can't be said for you and Nadine. That girl practically swallows her breakfast in one bite."

Emilia's gaze narrowed a little as she sat up in her bed, "I am surprised. The diary is back, which means you know everything, so what brings you so in here? How come you have nothing to say."

Sophia closed her eyes for a moment, tightening the grip that she had on the bag, "I have so many things I need- I *will* tell you, but right now, it's breakfast time despite the fact that it's 14:00 o'clock. That, and...the fact that you saved us all. So for now, just get dressed, and let's go somewhere outside."

As the reality settled in, Emilia's smirk went upward, "I see you still haven't changed a bit. Even though I can see that you are mad at me as hell, you still care for my well-being."

Sophia lowered her gaze a bit, sighing deeply, keeping her calm demeanor. "Just do as I said," with that, she left the room, leaving Emilia staring at her diary.

At the end of the day, it doesn't matter if she ever forgives me.

Since Nadine was relaxing in her own room, which she assumed her brother was doing the same in his own, Emilia left with Sophia as soon as she got in some warm hoodie, walking with her down the path that she was not particularly sure where it would lead them.

The weather was rather chilly, considering the fact that it was June, but then again, it was never that warm on this island. She didn't mind, though. She enjoyed the chilly breeze of the soft wind hitting her cheeks.

Neither of them spoke during the walk. The air between them was filled with pregnant silence since that was ready to give birth to an awkward conversation.

"This looks like a good place to eat." Sophia suddenly broke the silence as she pointed to the clean (from rocks) spot near the small cliff on the shore. It was relatively close to the village but not close enough for them to be disturbed.

Disturbed from what?

I am the only disturbing thing on this island.

For once in her life, Emilia obeyed Sophia's wishes, placing the blanket on the spot that her partner mentioned, sitting on it in Buddha style, facing the ocean that was slightly sprinkling them here and there. For a moment, she thought of the fact that she didn't deserve to be caressed by the little things that make life worth living.

The ocean, however, did not agree, and neither did the breeze.

Sophia sat next to her, her own food untouched on her knees. Before taking a bite, she smiled lightly at Emilia, "Don't eat that fast. You don't need a stomachache with everything else."

"You...said the exact same thing to me on that day." Emilia finally looked up, taking a small break since her last bite was a little too big. She didn't care as much for the taste.

My mouth is not as big as my ego.

The brunette made a small "o," nodding.

Taking another bite of her own sandwich, Sophia passed the pepper to Emilia, but she refused the offer. The brunette narrowed her eyes, looking at the ocean as she indulged in her own food. She didn't recall the last time she had eaten a ham sandwich. The time...before Emilia's return was filled with surviving, and sometimes, it was easy to fall into the routine, which would slowly cause even the smallest enjoyments to blur together. God, she loathed the daily routines.

Considering the heaviness of everything that they had to unpack, the pregnant silence was bigger than ever. Neither of them seemed to mind it during the breakfast (which was technically brunch).

.

.

When both of them finished with their food, they still stayed on the blanket, a slight breeze caressing them as they stared into the sea that was ever so lightly kissing the sky.

"God, Em, I wish I could hate you."

"That's understandable," Emilia answered nonchalantly.

"Who the hell do you think you are? A Goddess? I acknowledge that I will never be able to fully understand your pain but who the fuck gave you the right to- to-" Sophia stood up furiously, at which Emilia noticed that her little idiot was clutching her own firsts, visibly furious, "To play with people's lives, not knowing any of the circumstances that led them to do any of it, and...to have this moral high ground...to decide who lives and who dies?!"

Ever so slightly, Emilia turned to the ocean once again, trying to lose herself more in it. She was able to understand that any human being in Sophia's position would detest all of Emilia's actions because, in the end, that's precisely what Emilia was.

A hyper-ambitious monster with no home.

"Me. I don't regret it one bit."

The brunette let out the best of her current emotions, falling onto the blanket afterward.

For a moment, Emilia continued sitting still, shocked.

Did Sophia just slap me?

"How dare you?! You got your revenge! This...is just something out of this world. Just stop." Sophia said through a few sobs, letting it out, her emotions dripping in her words as well as her tears, "Don't give yourself excuses that you are doing it for me or your brother... Perhaps, that was your initial motivation, but at this point, I can't really imagine it's for the world."

"..."

"You didn't just get your revenge. Your mind got corrupted with revenge against...well, everything. At some point, you started just losing yourself more to it. But-" The brunette wiped away her tears, a determined look in her eyes, "It's enough. This is enough. You are just hurting yourself with this. Please, Em...for once, listen to me, and stop this madness."

For a second, her red-headed partner genuinely contemplated the offer, but the reality was different.

"For once, let me be selfish. *I* need you more than the world itself. You were right; you have always been right. This world is fucked up to no repair, so...why bother?"

"Because, at this point, my biggest sin would be failure. Do you think I do not know that creating a world like I have imagined is impossible?" Emilia noticed the sudden jerky movements of her left leg as well as her left hand, her body slightly shaking, "Do you think I do not know any of that now? But even so, how can I justify any of it without any results. At this point, I swallow the sleeping meds like candies, and they barely work."

She ignored the light stream of tears that slid down her face whilst Sophia watched in bewilderment, sympathy, and pity. Worried overflowed her, and her inner nurse kicked in back; she suppressed all of that to allow her partner to fully express herself, to allow her to fully be inside that Chinese wall that she had around her.

No, even the Great Wall of China palled in comparison to Emilia's inner defenses.

"I can't allow myself to die knowing what kind of world Rocky would live in...or you. So yes, I don't regret anything. Everyone else can die for all I care. *I* would rather die than give up on my dreams, no matter how selfish or inhumane they might be." Her jerky movements slowed down until they fully stopped as Sophia contemplated everything. She didn't miss the obvious that Emilia was hiding like a snake would a tail.

Something was deeply wrong with not only Emilia's mind but her body as well.

After taking a sigh, Emilia's little idiot approached her, taking all of her in one tight hug, "What on earth gives you the confidence that you can save everything that you care for? And even so, who is gonna save *you* at the end?"

With her ever so sleight hands, Emilia buried her face deep in the brunette's neck, taking in her vanilla scent, which sparkled something deeply buried in Emilia's mind and body, like a dying flower that finally got a taste of clean and fresh water.

She never really admitted just how much she only wanted Sophia to be next to her, just next to her, no matter the status of their bond, but needed her in every sense of the word.

After all, Sophia was a Yang to her Yin.

She always has been.

Chapter 24

Even after a month of their life on the island, Nadine would still wake up each morning, hoping that everything was just a big bad joke that Dad had made.

Hoping that she would see his bright and cheerful face, that wide smile, that she would be able to run to him, to hug him, and to whine, *"Daaaad! C-mon! Killed by a robot? Such a lame joke."*

It would not be far-fetched; despite his practical mind, he was a dreamer at heart just as much as her, and science fiction was his favorite genre – apart from horror and comedy, they always shared loved for those.

Heads, hands, legs flying around, and a pool of blood was not something that ever fazed them. They would always just laugh at the absurd stupidity of characters in horror movies – sure, going to the dark room, alone and weaponless, where the killer might be – makes total sense.

After all, in a sleepy mode in the mornings, it was easy to take in her surroundings and to see that all of her belongings were right there with her, only to see her hopes being crushed by the position of the window, by the fact that the cocoa that Dad would make was not waiting for her, and that the smell of a delicious breakfast would not wake her up.

She wasn't a believer; how could she ever possibly be, but at times, she prayed to the God that she didn't believe in for everything to really *be* a joke. That her Dad would be there when she messaged him, that at least, only once, she would hear his voice again.

That she would be able to teach him at least once why it was important to reply fast – a lesson he gave her so many times when he would message her without her responding quickly and then him thinking of the worst.

Clenching her jaw as she hid her sobs in the fetal position on the bed, she stared at the tiny crack in the wall, immediately imagining that her Dad would notice it the moment he stepped in the room, telling her he would fix it.

Just like how he always had a solution to everything whenever she had a problem – always being there to fix each and every single one of her problems, no matter how big or small.

She didn't want to cry. She despised the fact that she was crying.

If her Dad really were there, he would hug her, patting her back ever so slightly in a comforting way, telling her that nothing would ever be worth her tears.

But she would disagree. He was very much worth her tears.

She knew crying would not bring him back, but she couldn't hold in every single negative emotion she had. She needed an outlet. She was just too young for any of this.

That thought alone made her bawl even more, and she sobbed harder, knowing very well that she would never ever hear those words again. Knowing that she would never again taste any of the

meals that he would so happily make only for her (and for himself –
she chuckled at that thought), knowing that he would not be there
for any of the following big events in her life.

She really didn't want to cry.

But nothing on the planet would be able to stop the tears
flooding her cheeks as her sobs slowly died out.

Another thought crossed her mind – the irony of the fact that
science fiction was his favorite, and then his life ended so suddenly
at the hands of a robot.

She bitterly smiled, her head slightly pulsating due to the
pressure and stress (another reason not to cry – he would say).

At the very least, he died as a hero.

*Dad, how badly I wish I had hugged you more. How much I wish
I had told you how much you meant to me.*

*I just…I wish I had told you that you have always been my biggest
hero.*

Fuck Spiderman or Superwoman.

You're always going to be the best hero to me.

She turned around, hoping that at least the psychical numbness
in her body would go away quickly but deep down, knowing the
state and progress of her chronic illness, she knew that hope could
only do so much, and in order to get better (as much as she was able
to), she would once again need to turn off the stress, and in a way,
become a robot just so she would be a better human.

Ha, the irony!

After all, the fucking stress was the biggest source of misery for
her. So just loosen up, and relax! No stress!

But no matter how much colder of a person she became…how
does one become a robot?

Life would always throw some sort of stress at you.

But, I will live.

I always would.

She noticed another side of her body getting painful aches all over, as though she was in a sea of a thousand hot needles - a curse of her everlasting illness. She remembered her younger days when she found out about everything. She was how old...ten-eleven? Eh, it didn't matter anymore.

At first, her days were blended with denial and then grief seasoned with pity - *why me?*

It never seemed fair, and in a way, she would be mad at the world and everyone who she did not care about their health or ruining it on purpose - those who smoke or drink to obliviation.

"They might as well as just die - they don't know how to enjoy life." She recalled writing in the diary at some point, "Those pathetic weaklings that don't know how to deal with life."

Perfect health or at least the decent one; she would kill for it without a second thought.

Perhaps, that was why murderers never fazed her. Deep inside, she was never sure what she would do if given a chance for something that was so brutally taken away from her.

And then, little by little, that monster of a disease would slowly eat her alive until she wondered if life was really worth a fight.

In the corner of her mind. she used to have a detailed plan to just leave this world - in a way, a silent and perfect suicide. After all, wasn't she going to be a burden to everyone, especially her father, for the entirety of their lives?

She could not bear to be a parasite. She really would rather...just die. Sure, some people would be hurt initially, but they would eventually move on.

After all, that was life. It always moves on. It didn't matter whether you were there or not.

As much as her inner child would beg her not to, the crippling idea was there every single time she passed the riverside on her way back to school.

She really was too young for those philosophical questions – so life smacked the maturity right into her face, knocking out her inner child in the process.

"But then I would remember the times that life would caress me."

And so...she would skip reality by watching different anime. Indulging herself in different fantasies was her soul medicine. She would see her favorite characters always fighting, proving their strength, and reaching their goals even when all the odds were against them.

Nadine was a narcissist, in a way, and would always think of herself as the main character in life (which was one of the biggest reasons she would always dye her life probably as long as she was alive – the basic colors were, god forbid, out of questions).

Slowly, the little voice in her head would say that she was that main character in anime, that she was stronger than that monster inside her. That she can, and she would beat that monster.

No, no, she would beat *everyone* in the game we call life.

She would become the most successful person despite everything being against her (well, apart from her Dad – she knew he was her biggest fan; he always was).

"Thanks, daddy." She whispered, wiping her tears, still in her thoughts of her younger days.

And so she set it out as her biggest goal in life. To beat everyone - to prove everyone wrong. She would not allow anything to stop her.

The pity that people used to show her would turn into admiration and inspiration for those to come. It would be her legacy.

And so, the said curse, later on, became a blessing in disguise with so many little personality traits that were little life blessings and products of the said curse.

As well as her biggest gift - limitless imagination. That's why she was writing or coming up with stories for as long as she could remember. One world was not enough for her needs.

And so she broke free of her own pity party and saved her own life.

After all, giving up was never in her vocabulary.

And with that, the comatose inner child woke up, finally having a chance to live and breathe with full lungs. She never stopped them, either. She would just encourage them with a big grin on her face, finally finding enjoyment in the senseless life.

Just like that child, she decided to get up from the bed, wiping away her tears in the process. She had to find a way to move on, even if life was more senseless now than ever before.

The petite girl was washed over with many symptoms of instability and physical weakness, but she managed to slowly enter the living room, where she was met by Emilia's brother.

The handsome young man turned around his head from the couch and offered her a small smile.

"Fancy drinking some tea?" he held up his cup as Nadine shook her head. She appreciated the fact that he didn't ask about her red, teary eyes.

She sat next to him, sighing a few times to regain her energy, barely enough just to have enough mental clarity for any conversation.

"There's something I want to talk about with you. I just didn't have a chance." He took a sip of his tea as she flipped through the channels, searching for some sort of entertainment.

"I know that your father was involved in the group that Emilia is a leader of, and I may not know much, not because I do not care, I *care*, it's just Emilia keeping me in the dark, but she is not a bad person. I have no idea what she is doing, but I do trust the fact that she is not a bad person. On the flip side, she is not the best one either." He let out a heavy sigh, abandoning the small wooden cup in front of them, "Sometimes, I think it's harder to be her than to be with her."

Nadine looked at him from the corner of her eyes, "I know. I don't know her a lot, but she reminds me of...me. She is so deep inside her own little world that she just cannot accept the fact that sometimes, just sometimes, she is not right and that she needs others. The world didn't isolate her. She isolated herself. That's...at least what I gathered from the few conversations we have had so far. And bits from Sophia."

The young man nodded, looking surprised, "You are very insightful."

Nadine glanced at the TV once again, realizing that the news was rather serious, so she quickly turned up the volume, listening to it carefully.

"...and with that, the new world conflicts have escalated to the worst scenario. The third world war has officially started. We urge the citizens to stay safe as we enter the new era..." with that, Nadine zoned out, blinking a few times rather too slowly. Did she just hear that correctly?

Oh, what the hell...

Like my life makes any sense whatsoever.

It was never fair in the first place.

Was it fair...he would still be alive drinking tea with me in our backyard.

I will live. After all...I have to. I already saved my life many years ago.

The man next to her sat silent for a few minutes until he finally broke the silence rudely, "I really didn't think it would come to *that*. I mean, there are always some conflicts happening around the world, but this?"

Something crossed Nadine's mind as she turned to Richard, "Didn't you say that Emilia, as unpredictable as she is, decided to get in here suddenly? Could it be...that she knew something? And my dad! He was killed by a robot! So Emilia had a destabilizer."

The man furrowed his eyebrows in thought, "That's plausible, but we can't say enough for sure. However, we will have to speak to Emilia soon. She must have known something. At least more than your average person that would only find about this on the news."

Speaking of the devil...

Emilia entered their house as if on cue, with Sophia following behind her. They were soaking wet, probably from the sudden rain.

Two pairs of eyes met the green ones, and Emilia looked confused, not sparing a glance at the TV.

"What on earth is your involvement in the third world war?"

"Excuse me, what the fuck, brother?"

Sophia stood awkwardly, not sure whether to be in the living room or go to the bathroom, considering the fact that both of them were soaking wet, and her nurse instincts were kicking it that they would get sick if not treated.

Richard stood up abruptly, slightly glaring at his sister. "I am sick of this! I want answers. Ever since...*that* you don't ever tell me anything. I always find things about you on my own. Em..." he sighed deeply, his eyes pleading a little, "I am no longer a child."

The red-headed averted her eyes to the other side, anywhere, just so she would not need to face her brother, "I guess it's official. After all, I had no way of keeping this a secret forever." She decided to sit down on a green couch in their "living room" next to Nadine, who kept her head bowed. "All I ever wanted to was to protect you, Rocky. I just wanted to protect the people that I had grown to care for from everything. In retrospect, I wanted to prevent the Third World War from actually taking place during the course of our lives. Everything that I have been doing for a while now was towards that goal. That's my only involvement in that."

Emilia's eyes became gloomier, and she glared into her palms, her lips shaking a little, "But even my very best was not enough. I have sold my soul and my last piece of humanity to make this world a better place for you but now...I have failed, and I am left with nothing but bloody hands and sins that even a devil would be ashamed of!" she clutched her hands, and suddenly she realized that the miserable laugh was slowly building up inside her as hopelessness danced in her mind.

As her laugh echoed in the place they called home, everyone stared at Emilia apart from Nadine, who just put her hands inside her oversized hoodie.

As the echo of her laughter dried out, the miserable devil stood up, going to her own room as silence filled the room.

Chapter 25

As soon as Emilia entered her room, tears started pouring down her cheeks for the first time in a while.

It was okay, though. No one could see them.

I failed.

"What's there left to do..." she murmured to herself, mindlessly approaching the closet with a key locket. She unlocked it with a key that was inside her pillowcase and opened the closet wide. Her eyes immediately locked on the pile that was covered with a white rug.

She wasn't sure whether her knees gave up on her or she gave up on them, but she soon found herself on the floor, staring at the rug. Her hand, now shaky due to her physical issues, pulled the rug abruptly down, revealing the medium-sized machine onto which there were two glass-looking containers filled with liquid.

"Hey, mom and dad...it's me." Emilia wiped away the tears, her eyes looking soulless as she stared right into the two brains that were inside the liquid containers.

She sighed deeply, and as though they truly were there, she hugged the machine with all she had, "I am sorry I failed. I failed at everything."

"Not really. You fucking saved all of us, you big doofus."

Emilia tensed and immediately let go of the machine as she soon found out that it was Nadine that had entered her room (and even closed the door after her, she noticed mindlessly).

"Don't worry. No one is going to see you crying apart from me...and" she glanced at the machine, "them."

"What do you want?" Emilia said annoyingly, "I just want to be alone. I have always been better off alone."

"Same." Nadine sat in Budha style right next to the red-haired woman, "Which is why I locked the door after me. You don't want anyone to see you crying coz crying has always been a weakness in your own eyes. And the world is rough, so you gotta be rougher than the world."

Emilia smirked for a split second, letting out a small "hmmm." Perhaps this kid was more similar to her than she'd realized.

It takes one to know one.

"You know...I barely know you, but I really do not think you are a bad person. You just convinced yourself that you're bad enough. Perhaps, you are not the best one either, but hey...you saved not just my life, but Phia's and your brother's as well. That gotta count for something...."

Out of the blue, the petite girl hugged Emilia, who just sat there shocked, "You don't have to place the burden of the whole world only on your shoulders. I...I know how it feels, but you're only hurting yourself if you don't allow anyone in. Yes, not everyone is a good person, but not everyone is a bad person either."

"What are you suggesting? For you to help me?" Emilia said as Nadine let go of her.

The petite girl shook her head, "Nope. You are like me. You aren't capable of fully trusting others, and you never will be. You don't trust nobody. But, interestingly enough, all of us trust you."

"..." Emilia sat silently, not sure what to say.

"What I am trying to say is that...you have to let someone or something in just enough so it would give you inner peace. Just so it would be your one true home. You deserve a bit more from life itself."

As soon as those words left Nadine's mouth, it was as though the red-headed was suddenly plunged into the ocean of clarity of everything that could have been.

Emilia's gaze instantly locked with Nadine's innocent one as she muttered, "Apple".

I...was so deeply buried inside my own mind that I failed to see what was in front of me the whole time.

This whole time...as I was searching for the apple of my life, I just needed...to be selfish...just that one time...

That one time when everything could have turned out differently.

I failed to see what I needed because of what I thought I wanted.

I have been my own biggest enemy the whole time.

It wasn't anyone else. It was me who ruined my life.

"Apple?" Nadine looked both curious and confused at that, and she was pretty sure there was more to this fruit to Emilia than at first thought.

"I have always wanted more from life...Nothing was ever enough. But now I realize that the apple of my life has always been with her. God..." the red-headed explained rather vaguely as she closed her eyes in defeat. "Sophia was never weak in the first place. She moved on with the world to the best of her abilities whilst I was stuck inside my own delusions. I am...pathetic. Utterly pathetic."

I could never even move on from my parents' death...

I still can't accept that they aren't actually alive.

The petite girl sighed, carefully choosing her next words, "Not really. You have been trying to save everyone and everything on your own, including your parents. That's...enormous. Whilst I don't understand everything, I think you should first talk with Sophia. Seems like you two have some unfinished business. Actually, it had always felt like it when she talked about you."

"Fuck, no." Emilia glared at Nadine, "I know I would keep hurting Sophia. She is better off without me, and that's a fact."

"...Maybe so. But isn't it selfish of you to decide for her?"

"Not this time. I know her. She...god, she knows so much, and still...wants to save me."

Once again, the petite girl looked in confusion, "And why is that a bad thing?"

"Because I don't deserve salvation. And spare me the philosophical answers that everyone deserves equality and all that bullshit. That's all fine and dandy in theory, but in reality, this world would be just so much better without some people. Including myself."

I just...play game number.

If everything worked as I imagined, then I would have been the only bad one left.

"You know..." Emilia continued, staring into her parents, "It might be possible to get Emanuel's brain and-"

"I highly doubt my dad would want to live in a jar." Nadine interrupted and shook her head, "Just no. I..." she made a deep sigh, "I will live. I must live on."

The red-headed decided to simply nod, deciding it really was not her place to push any of it. Deep inside, she knew she was reviving them for all the wrong reasons, but she didn't care for morals as much as the girl beside her did.

That evening, Emilia couldn't fall asleep. She didn't even try with the meds since she knew nothing could possibly work, considering her present state of mind. When she thought everyone was asleep, she sneaked out in the middle of the night and went to the exact same spot she was in earlier the same day with Sophia.

She sat at the exact spot she had done, listening to the waves as she took in everything the ocean had to offer. She smiled at the temporary tranquility, letting her soul and mind wander around the darkness. It felt all too familiar every single time she did.

Just like the time I met Sophia...I still have no answers on that episode.

"Figured I would find you here. You're kind of a creature of habit at times." She heard a familiar voice that she wished she could have kept ignoring, no matter how lingering she felt.

Sophia made a spot next to her, not sparing her a glance.

"At this point, I don't know whether you believe me or not, but I truly wanted to stop the war from taking place. Perhaps I overestimated my ability, and...everything was in vain. Every scientist, politician, criminal...everyone that I have killed because I deemed it to be alright."

The brunette let out a deep breath, "I might be a little biased, but-"

"But what? At the end of the day, killing anyone is wrong but let's be fucking real here. How on earth is it beneficial for the current politicians to live with any of us? The criminals who do the unimaginable to those weaker than them, or scientists that play with people and animals as though they are not living beings at all? How the fuck are *they* beneficial to humans? To the world?

The animal world has better order than the human world. It's for a fucking reason. They kill those who are not worthy of living. It's so simple."

"Are you trying to make yourself feel better or convince me to give up on humanity just like you did?" the brunette replied calmly as the wind messed with her hair.

Emilia made a small tch sound, "Both. You don't know that so many smaller wars happened over the world as well. Groups from different nations, and sometimes the same nations, would send different robots against each other's citizens. I stole a few destabilizers years ago."

"The thingy you had that day at the graveyard?" Sophia asked to which Emilia just made a small nod.

"Yeah."

The brunette let out another deep sigh, still comprehending everything she was hearing, "You know...despite everything, you are still a hero in my eyes."

And a monster in my own.

Many would agree.

"A hero doesn't have this much blood on their hands." Emilia immediately replied in a harsh tone, staring right into brown eyes. How Sophia even sat, let alone trust her this blindly, was something she could never ever comprehend.

"I know...You have never been perfect, but you have always been perfect for me. Honestly, I always had thousands of reasons to hate you." The brunette's stern gaze fixed into now what appeared to be an abandoned meadow of intrigue, "You probably wouldn't even care. You never cared what anyone thought of you. But just because of that one kiss, not even a real one, for which, fuck you, I became a doll once again you could so easily play with. Just...damn you. Damn you, you gorgeous bitch."

Hold on.

Did she really just say all of that? Am I not dreaming?

That's literally admitting that she wants more.

But something inside Emilia writhed to go back to a safe space. Sophia was entering dangerous territory. She was uncertainly stepping into a place that Emilia, frankly, was not even remotely ready to touch yet. She probably was never going to be.

Once tactical, bland, and predictable, brunette apparently became bolder with age.

And so, she did the only thing that she could.

Turned off all of her emotions to the best of her abilities and replied in a rushed manner.

"Love is insignificant in my life. It's been fixed in my head for too long."

This time, it was Sophia that gave offered Emilia her own trademark smirk. "Why do you keep lying to yourself?"

"It's sort of an ego thing. You wouldn't understand."

This shut the brunette down a bit since it was a fact. It was the red-headed who was egotistical more than enough for both of them "...I want to."

"Why?"

Why? What the fuck can I possibly offer you?

The only thing I have at this point is everything that money can buy.

*But it's just not enough...Not for you, at least. It keeps **me** satisfied.*

However, is it ever enough?

The brown poles widened to the point where it was almost comical, as though she asked the question to the most obvious answer "Because I want you in my life. I need you in my life. It's only you who can push me to be free of my own boundaries."

"…"

The deep-rooted silence settled between them as both of the women turned back to the unsettling ocean.

How on earth do I go from now?

I…can't do this. I don't do love. I don't know how to.

Besides, this world has been doomed from the very beginning.

Suddenly, both of the women were drawn to the fast-moving light in the sky, and as soon as Emilia realized it was a shooting star, she gasped a little, but the mere sight of that hope gave her the courage to reply with a small smile on her face.

"You're an idiot."

I want a better ending in the next life. God, Universe, something, please make me meet her a little earlier.

Give me a little more hope and sensitivity in the next one coz, in this one, it's already late for this one.

"But I am your idiot."

With that, Emilia turned to the other side just so Sophia wouldn't be able to see the glassy eyes she had.

You always will be.

Chapter 26

For some time, they just sat there, neither of them really wanting to leave the other one yet never ready to even touch the other one.

They just sat with the ocean, taking in all of its tranquility as the wind danced around, and nothing except the waves could be heard.

Not even the moonlight was befriending them since it was occupied with the dark clouds. It would probably rain very soon.

"You know...I still have some questions. Whatever happened to Alice? Alice...Stein, was it? The assistant? If I recall correctly, it was said that she killed herself, but then you mentioned...that pushing her over the edge was easy...and yeah."

Emilia grunted and decided to lie down on the ground, the tiredness already taking over her.

"Ah, I always knew something was off about her. That was one of the few times I hated the fact that I was right." She closed her eyes for a moment as though she was researching her own memories, "And I, despite the fact that I *get* it. I get why she did the things she did. I am no better. No, in fact, I am way worse."

Sophia stayed silent since this was something she didn't know about at all. Whilst Emilia's diary was a treasure, filling so many little details that just felt like badly-written plotholes, there were still some things that Emilia never wrote or explained in the diary. It was as though, sometimes, Emilia wanted to hide some things from herself as well.

Sophia was, however, not surprised by this in the slightest.

Everything Emilia deemed to be "weak" would be discarded, and that included her own feelings.

And everything that could not be discarded would have to be forgotten and swiped under the rug. Expect...at this point, Sophia was too tired to play that childish game of tugging the rug and searching for clues. She would comfort Emilia even if that cost her her own life. She was not the fool that she used to be when they were younger. And so, she would tell Emilia to, at the very least, tell her what was under the rug. Especially since she was involved with some of the biggest dirt.

Perhaps, Emilia matured in her own way as well. After all, she was the one who handed her the diary, and she was the one who initiated answering all the questions she had.

Emilia continued, "Alice didn't have the happiest past. In fact...I don't think she ever fully developed her own personality since she was just always living in surviving mode. She never met any of her family. She spent more time going from orphanage to orphanage than actually living anything remotely similar to a 'normal childhood.' She was...always a loner. She was worse than I had ever been. Then one day, a miracle happened. She got adopted by a wealthy couple of altruists. Finally, she had a place that she could call home. A place where she might belong."

Sophia stayed silent, waiting for Emilia to continue. She didn't fail to notice that her partner was having health issues, but she knew that the very fact that she was talking so *openly* was rare and that any *other* concerns would have to come later – she needed to be selfish this one little time.

Em was a big girl. She would live.

After taking in a deep breath, her partner continued, "After only two months, a burglar managed to break in during a power outage. The only survivor was Alice. All of that took place before the age of 10. So instinctively, she was sent back to the orphanage since there was no will or anything which she could use."

Sophia interjected, "She, however, was a professional in her field. Your dad was only working with the best people."

"True. Despite everything, she still excelled academically. In a way, it was her way of coping and actually having something for herself. That, of course, was only enough as long as the scholarship was covering everything, and then when she graduated, the reality of this world hit her. Finding a job was easy but sustaining a decent life was the biggest obstacle. Inflation, poverty, lack of resources...you know. The usual shit."

Emilia let out a small yawn and, once again, laid on the ground with her hands underneath her head, "And so, Daniel used that to his advantage. She was already so vulnerable and hopeless. They had never met face to face, so it was Ronald who approached her with...the job offer. As long as she does everything as told, without asking any questions, she would get paid nice money. He used her desperation and made a perfect follower out of her. She never had to kill anyone herself; just get info here and there, duplicate keys, play a role of an assistant...."

The brunette made a small nod, noticing that Emilia trailed off, probably remembering the event that turned her whole life upside down. Sometimes, just sometimes, Sophia wondered what would have happened with the two of them if Emilia never lost her parents, if Daniel never entered their life, and if Emilia's biggest problem remained being kicked out of university.

But instead, the universe played and toyed with the two of them, and the most unimaginable things happened. Some of which were impossible, statistically.

Sometimes, and only sometimes, she wondered whether the universe was broken. Was there anything she could do to prevent some of the miseries that have happened thus far?

But...if Emilia couldn't, then what could she possibly do? After all, Emilia took care of her job. Sophia recalled the days when she was accepted into her dream job, and not just that! Her working hours were exactly as she wished, and her salary was enough to support her and her mother. Back then, she just thought it was her hard work, all that volunteering, and basically, just the universe paying her back.

But that couldn't be further from the truth.

All of that was Emilia bribing her boss, pulling some strings here and there.

Emilia was the one taking care of everything, and not the Universe.

The first time she found out about it, she was not sure how she felt. After all, she wanted to at least try to take care of herself but...in the end, it was Emilia who did the hard work. And even if she when wanted to be angry at her for meddling so much in her life and then disappearing right when she needed her the most (or just maybe, get her away from that cannibal!), what could she possibly be angry for?

Emilia literally gave her everything she wished for and didn't even ask for anything in return.

"It took me a while to find out the whole story, but funnily enough, Daniel was more chatty than I imagined him to be. Perhaps...it was because he didn't think he would live, but I... just couldn't....and didn't want to. Part of him was always done with humanity, and ending everything would be an easy way out. However...he was also just a fucking kid. It's like, for a split second, I saw a very broken version of my brother in him. As for Alice, I already told you. I used her guilty consciousness and pushed her over the edge of something she already wanted to do her whole life."

Sophia sighed deeply, knowing she couldn't add anything to help remove the skeletons from Emilia's closet. They have there for too long, and the only thing she could do was to accept it no matter how fucked up everything was. But then again, in a world like this, Emilia wasn't the worst one either.

Sure, she isn't the best one either, but still.

Em is Em.

"I still have so many questions...About Daniel, about you, about us being kidnaped, so many missing pieces."

"I already said so much, but then again, it's the least I can do. I always keep my promises." Emilia yawned once again, "So shoot."

The brunette lay next to Emilia, mimicking her position, "Tell me more about the case. Why did Daniel do what he did?"

"Because he wanted to see someone else experiencing worse misery than him. He didn't want to be alone after all. The people he killed around the world were selected at random at first. I was right back then about it...Demon wants to see people break down, so that's why he ordered those murders. He wanted to see someone else more desperate than him." Emilia cleared her throat, "He was no better than Alice in a way. So stuck in his own desperation that he needed others to join that doom. And so, random killings were not *good* enough. He was not only active in Germany but in other places as well. He would have different men kidnap and toy with his victims."

Toy...how?

Sophia wasn't sure she wanted to know the answer to that question, but she needed to get to the bottom of everything.

"Remember when my dad worked on the case and mentioned that there was something off with victims' faces? Turns out that, before the victims were killed, they would have shown edited photos or videos of their loved ones dying whilst, in reality, those loved ones would be completely safe and untouched – most of the time. Sometimes, he really would kidnap people and then select their closed one to...you know. That perhaps answers your question of why they were kidnapped and taken so far away. This also solves some other cases of missing people as well. They would be kidnapped, brought somewhere else, and then toyed with. We were...lucky to have gotten away in the first place. That is...you were luckier. Your mother wasn't one of the selected people like my parents were. That could be kinda dad's fault for choosing to be a detective in the first place."

You wanted to be one as well.

You always followed in your father's footsteps, no matter how much you denied it. You saw yourself in him more than you ever wanted to admit. His weaknesses were your weaknesses as well. You just lied enough to yourself to the point where you truly started to believe your own lies.

Perhaps life was a bitch more to you than you have ever been.

"As to why some people were tortured with 'real photos' and some not, it's because he wanted to see the real pain. The real desperation. The fake one wasn't good enough. Although...I looked into the profiles of the people that were kidnapped, and there was one thing they all had in common. They all had that...edge to fight. They were all people like me. Loners who didn't care too much about the world...."

Why the fuck you continue lying to yourself more than anyone else.

You care too much for the world. That's why you're where you're.

"When I finally managed to track him, I never let him know it was me all along. I had a mask and a voice changer. He truly thought I was dead when I "died". Perhaps, he really thought no one could be worse than him. But then, I appeared and "chose" him to be my follower in return for his own safety...from me. At the time, I was surprised to see he just...followed me and obeyed everything so perfectly. You could say I was worse than the Demon himself. I did things...on a much larger scale. Daniel had Ronald doing all of the executions for him. He didn't enjoy pulling a gun. Me, however...I still remember the thrill of getting revenge against Ronald and ending his life with my own two hands."

Emilia pulled one of her hands up, smiling to the sky, taking a small break from talking so much, "The group that I lead...led had three members. Daniel, as the executor, that Russian girl who helped us on the boat whom I found when we were kidnapped as the hacker, and lastly...Emanuel, the insider, Nadine's father. I didn't even have to force any of them. I simply offered them an opportunity. Daniel's killing was, in a way, my way of punishing him for everything. He had no problem consuming people, but he wasn't a fan of killing them. It would always reawaken the greatest pain and pleasure in him. That Russian girl, and no, I don't know her name, and I don't care, was happy to just continue helping me as long as she was paid on time...desperate life, I guess she had. And lastly, Emanuel. Well, what can I say except that he was the best father in the cruelest world you could think of. In a way, he reminded me of my dad...."

....

Damn, that's a lot to process.

Chapter 27

Both of them lay there for some time. Emilia started drifting into sleep at some point, and it felt like nothing could wake her up at that point. Not the loud waves, not the howling of the wind that played with Sophia's hair, nor the cold night.

However, as usual, Sophia's inner nurse instincts kicked in, and she felt the need to wake her up so they would go inside. She really didn't want a lung disease, thank you very much.

But, after Emilia bombarded her with so much info, she wasn't sure how and where to start processing it.

Every single thing that had happened was so tangled, and nothing felt like reality.

It was as though the reality was too much to handle, and her brain was telling her to stop thinking and just...jump into nothingness. She didn't have to think. She could just...*be*.

This is why she drifted into a deep sleep so quickly without any regard for anything else.

Chapter 28

“Bloody hell, what on earth are you two doing here?”

Not sleeping anymore, that's what.

Emilia slowly opened her eyes which wasn't for too long considering that the sun blinded her immediately.

Soon enough, she was met with the familiar eyes of her brother, staring right into her. He seemed to be annoyed a little, but Emilia didn't care enough at the moment. Lately, she noticed she was not caring a little too much.

“I guess we fell asleep talking. I am sorry we made you worried.” Her partner quickly interjected, which made Richard sigh.

“It's alright. I am just a little on edge about everything.”

“We are safe as we possibly could be on this island. It's the most isolated one. Plus, we have a bunker.” Emilia said crankily as she stood up, not caring that her clothes were a little dirty.

“...I know. I just...I don't want to be ungrateful, but I just imagined life to offer more than this.” Richard said, “But it is what it is.”

God...that's why I can't give up even though I already know I failed so miserably.

The rest of the day went pretty silently. Despite the fact that Sophia still had some unanswered questions, her brain hurt after processing everything that Emilia had told her the night before.

With that in mind, Emilia was left alone since Richard was religiously watching the news about the ongoing events as Nadine isolated herself in her own imaginary world. Usually, solitary was her life companion, but now...it didn't help her.

With no group to lead and no goals to conquer, she realized that her disease was progressing quite rapidly...too rapidly. Energy was leaving her body way too quickly, the spasms got worse, her eye did a little tango here and there, and a weird form of slight paralysis was affecting her. Not yet to the point where she couldn't move her muscles, but...it terrified her a little too much, which is why she was both surprised and happy (if happiness was still something she was able to feel) when she heard a light knock on the door. A distraction was welcomed in any way, shape, or form at that moment.

As she opened the door, she saw a handsome middle-aged man (although it was hard to tell how old he really was) in a coat. The first thing she noticed was that the man wasn't even that particularly nicely dressed, but he was radiating confidence to the point where if even he were to wear an old pajamas, he would still rock it. He was slim and tall, and he was definitely a looker in his younger days.

"May I help you?" she said curiously, keeping her focus on his eyes. They were deep dark brown and intense.

He smiled ever so slightly and made a small nod, "First, I need to check whether I am speaking to the correct person. Emilia Wilson?"

!!!

"No need to be alerted. I guess you could say I am a friend. After all, I am the only man who could understand your work. It's simply brilliant."

His voice was a perfect balance of bold and soft. The more he talked, the more Emilia was confused and worried as to who this man was.

To the world, Emilia Wilson was dead, so how did he know her? Who was he?

He said he was a friend...the fuck?

"My dear, you simply must join me for a cup of tea and a talk. It's been rather boring on this island lately."

Why not? I should keep him close...until I find out what he wants.

"Sure, I don't have any plans. But I need to ask. Who are you?" she slowly closed the door behind her, not trusting the man enough to turn her back to him.

Whoever he is...I have the gun with me at all times.

The man let out a small chuckle, his body moving ever so slightly to the rhythm of his giggle, and Emilia froze in shock when she heard the name.

"Andreas Walter"

Chapter 29

How is this possible? This man should have been dead.

Where the hell was he then this whole time?

More importantly, how does he know me? What does he want from me?

Better yet, is he someone that is a threat to Richard, Sophia, and Nadine?

"Here we are," Andreas said as they approached an isolated part of the shore that was covered with lots of trees and some clearing. In the middle, she noticed a small picnic table and a chair on both sides.

"Thanks, I guess?" Emilia said weirdly, and it genuinely came off as more of a question rather than a statement. Honestly, she was hoping to find out where he lived on the island...for research purposes.

As he sat down, he offered her a small smile, "You seem slightly disappointed. Did you really think I would bring you to my place so that you know where I live? Ah, darling, I only trust myself to know that information."

As the red-headed sat down, she eyed the man once again. Knowing who this man was, she didn't care for the tea and cookies. She was hungry for the answers.

Andreas sat down in an elegant manner, giving her a fake plaster smile once again, "Let's skip the small talk, shall we? I know who you are, and you know who I am. Do please, take the tea. I wouldn't benefit from poisoning you."

Emilia continued staring into him, and she mentally cheered as she noticed him letting out a small sigh.

"I guess you won't be drinking the tea after all. Too shameful. But then again, I wouldn't trust myself in your position either."

"What precisely do you want from me? How...did you survive? I thought Daniel killed you years ago." She finally spoke as the small wind played with the strands of her hair. It was a pleasant day. Too shameful she was sitting with an unpleasant person.

Andreas smirked ever so slightly, arrogance playing at the tip of his tongue. "Kill me? Darling, I am the creator of the perfect human species, not some silly toy in his game."

"Toy...you do realize he had killed people for his own benefit?" Emilia said in a slightly surprised tone.

This time, the man grinned ever so slightly, and for a second, Emilia shivered.

"Just like you. What makes you think you have any moral high ground?"

Her heart started beating slightly faster, "I have never killed people for *my* own benefit. It was always for a better tomorrow."

"Death is death. Besides, someone like you thrives in power. Don't tell me you don't like the thrill of playing God or, rather, Goddess? Don't tell you don't miss the moments when you are truly resetting the world?"

Emilia shut her mouth and looked the other way, swallowing hard her own pride. She hated the fact that this man was right. He was reading her too easily, knew too much about her, and he was leading the game. As much as she was drowning in misery, she remembered the moments when she saw herself as a hero, even though she would end up with bloody hands and a dirty conscience.

"I wanted...want to help the world. I can't allow my brother, Sophia...and others to live in one like this. Daniel wanted to see it burn; I want to reset it."

"Fascinating. I knew you and I would see eye to eye." Andreas grinned even more and delicately took a sip of his tea, "You see, human suffering has always bothered me. How can I be a human if I ignore it? It pissed me off to no end that no one was doing anything about it. So many illnesses and death that can be avoided. So I studied genetics. More precisely, eugenics. Such a perfect theory. The one that can end so many miseries! But so many people frowned at it, seeing it as an idiotic sentiment. As though leaving your bad genes behind is any accomplishment. Even cockroaches can breed. It's nothing special. And so, I wanted to see how the perfect humans would turn out. I thought once people see my results, surely, they would start changing their minds. But, alas, I was too late, and my most promising candidate turned out to be such a weakling. Ah, I guess what? Daniel wasn't as nearly as perfect as I thought he was. He killed my impostor. Told you I don't trust people."

Emilia blinked a few times as she clutched her hands, her mind processing everything. God, the man in front of her was messed up on so many levels, but she...she could see where he was coming from. She was no better than him in any way.

Just like her, he was using immoral means to reset the world.

The end justifies the means.

But to what extent?

"Daniel never thought of himself as perfect. He was a victim by design. So was his sister. You are one twisted man...but I am no better." She said as she clicked her tongue, "Scratch that. I am better. I *know* I am twisted. You, however, will easily dispose of others of their happiness just because you deem them imperfect for your new world. My new world would be open for anyone who doesn't cause harm to others."

"Spreading hereditary disease and high risk for illnesses onto another human being is not causing harm? Consciously putting that suffering onto your own offspring...I would argue that causing harm and plain is cruelty inspired by brutal narcissism and egoism."

"I can see where you are coming from, but you forget that suffering is the biggest inspiration for moving forward. If everything was perfect, then there would be no room for progress. Humans have come this far because of how imperfect we are. People used to die of common cold, and now we have so many medications. Their distribution is a problem, though."

"Then why don't people use their old phones and just keep upgrading them to solve the old issues. Why do they buy new ones? Because, darling, perfectionism is the key to everything."

"You just like to play God."

"So do you. You know, we are a perfect match, my darling. Perhaps, we might disagree on some grounds, but you understand the foundation of everything."

Emilia stood up slowly, biting her own lip, and placing her hands on the table, "You are so wrong. Take Nadine, for example.

The girl has so many issues, and still, she has a stronger will to live than anyone I have ever known."

Andreas smirked slightly once again, "My darling, that girl is just an exception. There are always exceptions. Way more people give up than truly move forward. Some of them would rather be dead than a dead weight, but they never voice it."

"Even so...you have no right to play with their lives like they mean nothing at all. It's their choice whether they live or die. They never chose to be sick or lack something."

"Which is why euthanasia should always be legal."

"Yes, if they are genuinely suffering from something, and there is no hope left. Your plan failed, though, so I will just let you believe you're a God or whatever." Emilia rolled her eyes and started moving from the table.

"Oh, my dear, but I already am." He replied, and the smugness in his voice was audible to the point where Emilia had to turn around and raise her eyebrows in confusion so she would prompt him to talk more, "I have been on this island long enough to fix it. Did you seriously think I could ever give up? Sure, it's not on a world scale, but we are currently in World War Three, so I am forced to rethink some details."

He...has "fixed" this whole island?

"You know, getting rid of the bodies on an island is quite easy, considering the sharks and all. Can be messy at times but oh well, people like me."

I don't

Once again, Emilia swallowed a lump in her throat, but this time, she had to swallow her own fear. This man was dangerous. Extremely dangerous.

To make matters worse, she knew she wasn't in the best shape; she was one of the people Andreas wouldn't just as easily feed the sharks as he was making breakfast.

"Fascinating. You look down at the rest of humanity, claimed to have never had faith in people, and yet..." he stood up from his own seat, making his way to Emilia, as he lifted her chin with this hand, smiling slightly, "You care too deeply. In fact, you care more than anyone. You're such a pretty little liar, my dear. You have managed to convince yourself of your own lies."

"Just what do you want from me?"

He grinned once again, his eyes turning colder every second, "The Russian girl you had in your team was quite something, wasn't she? I need her to get me some stuff. I want to take my project on a bigger scale."

"Why the hell would I help you?"

"You don't have to." Andreas moved his hand away, the corner of his lips still upwards, the authority in his voice never leaving, "I won't threaten your life. I know you don't really care about it at this point. I can see it. But, surely, it would be a shame if I called that woman you seem so fond of for a cup of tea. The cliff can be steep and very dangerous, you know."

He knows she is the weakest...the only one that can't save herself even if her life depended on it.

Without thinking, Emilia pulled the gun out, aiming at the man who didn't even blink an eye, and yawned at her movements.

"So predictable. If anything happens to me, you know what happens to Sophia. So what will it be? Do you care more for the world or her?"

...

Fuck

Suddenly, a feminine voice shouted, "Em! Don't help him! You can't let that monster win!"

She didn't have to turn around, but soon, the red-haired woman felt the familiar appearance next to her, "I heard everything. This time, I am going to make a choice instead of her. Just kill me."

"Ah, such a wasteful sacrifice for such an imperfect world. You really are an idiot." Andreas chuckled, staring into Sophia's eyes, who appeared to have grown imaginary guts to be bold like this. Perhaps, she had experience dealing with monsters.

You cunt. I can only call her that.

"But she is my idiot," Emilia growled as she narrowed her eyes at the man, spitting her words with venom. "And my final choice is easy. Sophia. I am going to choose her. I will choose her over the world without a doubt."

Does this make me a hero or a villain?

Or perhaps...just a fool?

"No! Em! You can't help him! You can't...can't do it! Just let him kill me." Sophia clutched her fists as she stared right into Emilia's eyes, who was still eyeing the man in front of them, "I know I am weak and pathetic, and all of their synonyms."

"You idiot! Don't you think I already know that?" Emilia growled through clutched teeth, still pointing the gun at Andreas, "But that time, I was selfless and let you go. I thought if I gave you everything, you could be happy. I truly let you go...but fuck it, it's not who I am. I am selfish. Have always been. So, this time, I am choosing you without a doubt in my mind."

"Such a fool." Andreas slowly lowered Emilia's gun down with a small smirk on his face.

"You...*bitch*! I am not worth the world! How the hell do you expect to go on living knowing what he plans to do?!" Sophia growled back as Emilia smirked, this time turning to her.

"You really seem to have grown some imaginary guts to talk back like that. I like it."

"I will be back. It seems you two have things to talk through." The man said, leaving with a small bow to both of them.

The brunette let the tears out in frustration, still clutching her fists. "I know I am not worthy of you or your kindness. But I will choose you without a single doubt in my mind. God, I need you. Fuck, the time I let you go, truly let you go, without keeping my tabs on you, you ended up in the hands of a cannibal. Very fucked up one, actually. But then again, he was just like a Lily, a creation, a victim by design. I guess we have an answer as to what happens when a creation goes wrong." Emilia made her way back to the table, staring into Sophia's eyes, "I am sorry."

Chapter 30

Emilia Wilson was everything but a person that says sorry. Not once has she heard her say that...until now.

"I am sorry."

Sophia made her way to the table, tears still sliding down her cheeks as she approached her red-headed partner, "You don't say sorry. Did your disease change your behavior as well? Don't think I haven't noticed. I am a nurse, after all."

"Like hell, I know." Emilia smiled slightly, both of them knowing very well that with the world ending, they might as well just be honest at this point. Andreas might as well just get back and get rid of them too. What was the point in hiding anything anymore?

The world was ending either way.

"You said you need me. Does that mean I am the only one who can save you from yourself? Restore your faith in humanity as a whole? Or maybe I am the only one who is crazy enough to be with someone like you?" Sophia sits right next to her, facing her with a small smile on her face.

No answer, but Emilia's self-mocking smile was enough of an answer for her. Perhaps deep inside, Emilia wanted to be saved just like she wanted to save the world. And Sophia was able to see that right through.

"When did you find out about me and Daniel?"

"When he got arrested, honestly. I was keeping my tabs on you, visiting your mother here and there...which she told you. But I thought if I truly let you go and focus on...my plan, you would be able to find your happiness...or something remotely similar to a normal life." Emilia sighed, recalling the memories, "Honestly, I found out because I got interested in the case and all that. I mean, he was literally testing the nerve theory on his victims. The last thing they feel before death, and how long would it be to stay on the corpse? That explains why the faces were so....gruesome. More than that, actually. Inhumane. Don't even get me started on the fact that he was eating good people to atone for his sins. Aaaand, in order to make himself feel better, he was literally serving the food of bad people at the restaurant to others to poison the core of other people. Seriously, you really do know how to pick people."

Sophia stayed silent and leaned her head on Emilia's shoulder, "It doesn't matter anymore."

Soon, both of them noticed the slight rain that was getting heavier and heavier with each passing drop which resulted in both of them running toward their little home. As soon as they entered and closed the door after them, she noticed that her brother was sitting on the sofa with a stoic expression on his face. He didn't even notice them at all.

Emilia was the first to approach him, so she would snap him out of his trance. Noticing the fact that her brother looked 10 years older, as though he had just heard about the world ending or something.

The third world war was already official. What could have possibly been worse than that?

Slowly, he shifted his gaze to his sister and smiled in pain. Soon, his words hit her like a brick to the fact, just like when they were kids.

"Em, big sister...tell me you can fix this?"

Those words were enough to erase all of the worries about Andreas, and her focus, her world, at that moment, was her brother. Her brother was a grown man, and as much as Emilia would always keep treating him like a kid (because, in her eyes, he would always be one), he kept saying that, proving to her that he was capable of taking care of himself. However, his expression, the agony in his words...

She knelt in front of him, took his hands in hers, and nodded, "Of course. *Anything* for you. What's the matter?"

He sighed slightly, still smiling in pain, his voice shaky, "They said there was a sudden disruption with the black hole. It's going to swallow the Earth in a matter of a day, maybe less."

. . .

This world...

This timeline...is just so doomed.

But why does it have to end this way?

Chapter 31

I *can't save us...*
    Everything will fall down...
Literally everything...
But then again, I have tried to build everything on such a shaky ground.

It's no wonder, though. So many unlikely things have happened one after another, but it was just doomed from the very start.

You win, universe. You took everything away.

How does one spend their last day on Earth?

Especially the one as messed up as this one? After all, they didn't even have many options. They didn't have time for...well, anything. And so, it was settled; they would just enjoy their last meal together. Those with appetite and those with no appetite.

It was a moment when truly nothing mattered. Every single plan they had was thrown away and would be swept away just like the whole Earth.

As they all sat on the shore on a blanket, looking at the sea that this time wasn't enough to provide its usual therapy. The wind was messing with them ever so slightly, the peak of nihilism keeping them all still and silent. Even the ever-so-chatty Nadine was down.

"If this is truly the end, then I am going to have my favorite meal." Nadine said as she dug into her pie with potatoes, "Perhaps, it might be for the better."

"Everything ending?" Sophia raised her eyebrow at the girl, confused.

"Well, think about it, so many nations have nuclear power, and...there would be so much more suffering. This way, everything ends fairly. No suffering, just end. At least I finished my book. I will do the manga in another life."

Richard took a sip of his tea, his face now dry from the tears, "In another life, I just want a normal life. I will settle down with normal everyday happiness. Having hobbies, a job, a wife and a kid, friends...it would be more than enough."

Emilia smiled slightly and took a big sip of her favorite tea, "In another life...another world, I hope to find someone way sooner. Or, at least, cross my path with her sooner."

"Oh, fuck it! Emilia Wilson, you gorgeous bitch, I lo-" Sophia was just about to grab Emilia's hand, but right before she even had a remote chance to finish her sentence, the darkness swallowed everything at the speed of light.

. . .

Nella, Nella, Nella...

Chapter 32

Have you ever woken up and felt that something was utterly wrong with....everything?

The reality was just...not quite right.

And no matter the reasoning, it didn't sit right where it's supposed to be?

And yet...

Everything was how it normally would be?

So misplaced, yet so right?

Emilia grunted, and before she even had a chance to open her eyes, she heard her mother calling her to get the water from the well.

Ah, right. She almost forgot that it was her turn to get the water to the house that day.

Opening her eyes, she was met with everything familiar yet so foreign for an unknown reason. It was her tiny room, that is, the room that she shared with her parents and her younger brother. It was her village, and the usual scent of animals could be felt from the window.

Nella,

Nella...

Phia...Sophia.

Why was that the name that she swore she had heard somewhere already?

Idiot.

I must be an idiot to even entertain that that dream must have meant something. I probably have just spent way too much time in the sun.

But...

Then why I can't shake off this feeling or longing for something?

...

Nella, we are so doomed.

I am so sorry.

Nella, I promise.

I have nothing left to give.

But-

I will find the perfect ending.

I will fight until the end.

Even if it takes forever to find the end beyond this world.

Because I love you too.

Author's Note

We meet again, my dearest reader!

The book ended on quite a cliffhanger?~

Anywhooo, if you're reading this, then, my dear reader, thank you for coming such a long way with me! Working on this book series has been quite a journey so far, and truthfully, I can't wait to start writing on the book 4!

I also want to thank everyone who supported me thus far; I know that I love to say that I only rely on myself but the support that I have had from the people close to my has been amazing. I must say 2022 has been quite an interesting year to me. I have been through quite a lot, and I also met some of the loveliest people as well. Very successful year as well.

But enough about me, my dear reader.

It's been raining today so make yourself a cup of tea, some cookies, and~

Do whatever makes you happy :D

Until next time~

Deja

EMILIA WILSON
WILL RETURN

For updates about current and upcoming
releases, as well as exclusive promotions, visit
the author's website at:
https://www.andreabedford.com

Don't forget to leave a review on store you get the book from. It
would mean a world to me! <3

Get a Free Copy of 'Deceive the World'

Your Free Book is Waiting

"Has it ever occurred to you that if you want to survive in this dark world, you have to become darkness itself?

Emilia Wilson was a typical, not so typical, 3rd-year college student who wanted nothing more than to pass all her subjects, read the books she had bought, and enjoy a good cup of her favorite tea in peace.

When she got a phone call from her parents to visit her Grandmother, who was at death's door, Emilia was pulled into the grand scheme of monstrous crimes, and the tea she wished for was nothing more than a long-forgotten dream.

Get a copy of the prequel

Deceive the World: Thorns of Life series here:

<u>www.andreabedford.com</u>[1]

---

1. http://www.andreabedford.com/

Also by Andrea Bedford

Thorns of Life Saga
Deceive The World
Fuck the World
Reset the World

Watch for more at https://www.andreabedford.com.

www.ingramcontent.com/pod-product-compliance
Lightning Source LLC
Chambersburg PA
CBHW021213160726
47994CB00001B/462

* 9 7 9 8 2 1 5 3 7 3 5 1 4 *